"[This book] should be on the shelves of all Canadi[ans] interested in the great explorers of their country."
– *Canadian Geographical Journal*

"This whole enterprise is to be highly commended si[nce] the key facts now reach the common reader . . . in [an] incisive, lively style." – *The Globe and Mail*

"Exceedingly informative." – *Western Producer*

"Shunning pedantry, [Mowat] proves his point . . . the Canadian past is not 'all old bones.' "
– *The Financial Post*

"[Mowat] has done an excellent job of 'freeing' Samuel Hearne from the 'cemetery of our years.' " – *Montreal Gazette*

"The greatness of Hearne shines through every page . . ."
– *Vancouver Province*

"Grippingly readable." – *The Montreal Star*

FARLEY MOWAT was born in Belleville, Ontario, in 1921, and grew up in Belleville, Trenton, Windsor, Saskatoon, Toronto, and Richmond Hill. He served in World War II from 1940 until 1945, entering the army as a private and emerging with the rank of captain. He began writing for his living in 1949 after spending two years in the Arctic. Since 1949 he has lived in or visited almost every part of Canada and many other lands, including the distant regions of Siberia. He remains an inveterate traveller with a passion for remote places and peoples. He has twenty-five books to his name, which have been published in translations in over twenty languages in more than sixty countries. They include such internationally known works as *People of the Deer*, *The Dog Who Wouldn't Be*, *Never Cry Wolf*, *Westviking*, *The Boat Who Wouldn't Float*, *Sibir*, *A Whale for the Killing*, *The Snow Walker*, *And No Birds Sang*, and *Virunga: The Passion of Dian Fossey*. His short stories and articles have appeared in *The Saturday Evening Post*, *Maclean's*, *Atlantic Monthly* and other magazines.

FARLEY MOWAT

COPPERMINE
JOURNEY

An account of a great adventure –
selected from the journals
of Samuel Hearne

M&S

An M&S Paperback from
McClelland & Stewart Inc.
The Canadian Publishers

An M&S Paperback from McClelland & Stewart Inc.

First printing February 1990
Cloth edition printed 1958

Canadian Cataloguing in Publication Data

Hearne, Samuel, 1745-1792.
Coppermine journey

(M&S paperback)
ISBN 0-7710-6690-2

1. Northwest, Canadian – Discovery and exploration. 2. Northwest,
Canadian – Description and travel – To 1821. 3. Hearne, Samuel,
1745-1792 – Journeys – Canada, Northern. 4. Indians of North
America – Canada, Northern. 5. Inuit – Northwest Territories.*
6. Natural history – Canada, Northern. 7. Great Britain – Exploring
expeditions. 8. Explorers – Great Britain – Biography.
9. Explorers – Canada, Northern – Biography. I. Mowat, Farley,
1921-   . II. Title.

FC3212.H4 1990   917.19'2041   C89-095149-7
F1060.7.H4 1990

Cover design by Pronk & Associates
Cover engraving of Samuel Hearne,
courtesy of the Hudson's Bay Company Archives
Cover line engraving of Eskimos from the holdings
of the Rare Books Division of the National Library of Canada
Interior map by Jack McMaster

Typesetting by S & G Graphics Inc.
Printed and bound in Canada

McClelland & Stewart Inc.
The Canadian Publishers
481 University Avenue
Toronto, Ontario
M5G 2E9

COPPERMINE JOURNEY

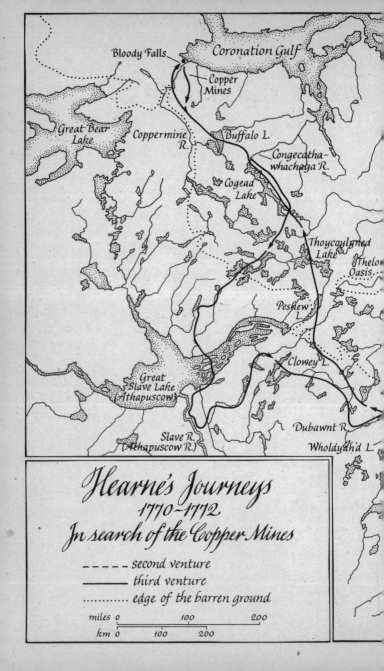

Bloody Falls

Coronation Gulf

Copper Mines

Great Bear Lake

Coppermine R.

Buffalo L.

Congecatha-whachaga R.

Cogead Lake

Thoycoylyned Lake

Thelon Oasis

Peshew L.

Clowey L.

Great Slave Lake (Athapuscow)

Slave R. (Athapuscow R.)

Dubawnt R.

Wholdyah'd L.

Hearne's Journeys
1770–1772
In search of the Copper Mines

– – – – – second venture
———— third venture
·············· edge of the barren ground

miles 0   100   200

km 0   100   200

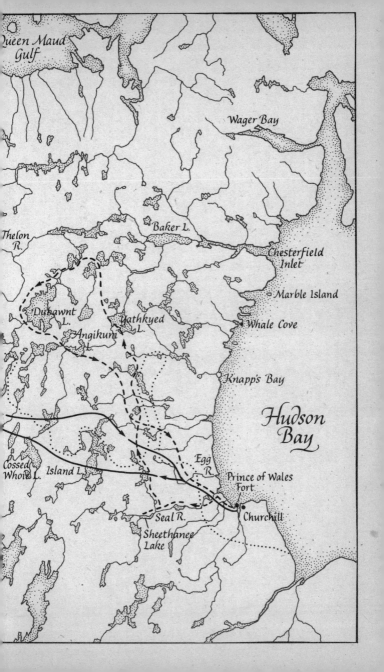

Foreword

ONE AUGUST day in 1947, Ohoto and I brought our canoe to a great lake called Angikuni, which lies in the heart of the Keewatin barren grounds. The sun beat down upon us with the furious intensity which it reserves for summer in high northern latitudes, and there was no escape from it, for the surrounding lands were as naked as a flayed carcass. We paddled slowly onto a windless bay and the uninhabited shores faded until we were faced by an illimitable expanse of pallid waters from which the massive sun had sucked all colour and vitality.

Far to the south a barren islet rose between two out-thrust arms of the receding mainland. The Eskimo suddenly raised his paddle. Pointing toward the distant reef, he cried, "There have been people at this place!"

Straining my eyes under the sun's glare I saw the talisman which he had seen. It was no more than a low pyramid of rocks, rising from a land of frost-shattered and malignant rock; yet it stood on the low back of the islet like a beacon fixed to reassure us in our loneliness.

We paddled hard toward it, and when we reached the shore we saw that many others had landed there before us. Through the millenniums the herds of caribou, which are the life blood of this land, had used the reef as a stepping-stone in their passage to and from the distant forests to the south. They had not always passed unscathed, for across the crest ran a line of up-ended granite slabs – rude semblances of men – stationed to turn the herds toward the hiding-places of archers who had been Ohoto's ancestors.

Clearly, the Eskimos of the inland lakes had been here once. But others had preceded them; for, wedged in a crevice in the rocks, we found a roll of brittle bark that had been cut from birch groves inside the forests' edge, three hundred miles away, and brought to this place by the almost forgotten tundra Indians.

We scaled the backbone of the islet to reach the pyramid. It was a squat cairn standing no more than six feet tall, and yet it dominated the world about us because, despite its substance, it was alien. It bore no kinship to the scant traces of themselves which native peoples have left upon the tundra plains. Beyond doubt it was the work of an outlander, and the proof was there, under a flat rock at the base of the cairn. I gathered that proof – some rotted fragments of a small oak casket – into my hands, and in that moment time dissolved.

I saw a vision of a white man trudging eastward over an endless plain, like a pariah in the wake of a band of nomad Indians who had cast him off. I saw him raise this symbol of his indomitable spirit upon an islet in an unknown lake. And in my mind's eye I watched him write a laconic description of his plight, before he once again took up the hard uncertainty of his survival.

I recognized him, since before our times only one Western man had ever ventured into the bleak wilderness that still bears the appellation which he gave to it – the Barren Ground. Some months earlier I had read this man's name, where he had engraved it with his own hands upon the grey rock at the mouth of Churchill River, on Hudson Bay. Unlike the vanished words in the cairn at Angikuni Lake, these have remained exactly as he carved them during an idle day, two summers before his great adventure was begun:

S^l Hearne
July ye 1, 1767

And it was indeed a great adventure. In the years from 1769 to 1772, he explored more than a quarter of a million square miles of the treeless plains which cap this continent. He was the first European to reach the mighty sweep of arctic coast which stretches westward from Hudson Bay to the Siberian seas. With no other company than that of reluctant and often hostile Indians, he walked close upon five thousand miles through one of the most forbidding territories in the world – a land so harsh that the last of his major areas of discovery was not revisited by white men until the 1920's. The hostility of the country and its peoples utterly defeated him twice over; yet he returned to conquer on his third attempt.

These accomplishments give something of his external measurements. They are spectacular enough, but they do not indicate the full stature of the man, for the smallest part of greatness in an explorer is his proficiency at discovering new seas and lakes, rivers and bays, mountains and plains. These things await inevitable discovery, for they are immutable. If they are not found in one generation, they will greet the next unchanged.

But the living features of an unknown country, those aspects which ebb and flow with the impermanence of life itself, these are the true revelations of the nature of new worlds. These are the aspects which the first beholder must seize on and preserve – not in a state of dead suspension, but in a state of life. To give some measure of immortality to these transient things requires genius. Hearne possessed it: he was able to defeat the years and to bequeath to us a living moment out of a vanished time.

He offered us this gift encompassed in the chronicle of his adventures which was published in 1795. Incredibly, it has been beyond the reach of ordinary men for more than a hundred years. Hearne's book has been re-issued only once, in 1911, when the Champlain Society published Dr. J. B. Tyrrell's edition. Unfortunately, that admirable work was limited to five hundred copies – for members of the Society alone. It very soon became almost as rare as Hearne's original. Perhaps this did not matter very much, for the Champlain edition was designed to preserve Hearne's relics with the full rites of scholarship, and not to give the rest of us free intercourse with a man imprisoned by our forgetfulness.

Not that I am belittling scholarship, as such. On the contrary, the exhumation of old bones and their assembly into some sort of order is an honourable and a useful task. My quarrel is with the fiction that the past is *all* old bones; for by giving assent to this fallacy we sanction the burial of our own greatness and we encourage the pedants and the historical dilettantes in the delusion that they alone are qualified to walk in the cemetery of our years.

I believe that this delusion, and this fiction, must be scotched. Furthermore, I believe that those well-guarded tombs, which hide our greatness from us, contain – not an array of pallid ghosts – but a concourse of living men possessed of such a superb and vital presence that their entombment becomes a reproach to all of us.

Samuel Hearne is only one of the giants we have buried alive, but he is one whom I would particularly like to free if I am able. Nor do I shrink at becoming a vandal in the sacred graveyard of the historians, in order to accomplish my purpose. Consequently, in the presentation of his own story, I have dealt ruthlessly with the funereal traditions of the academic method. I have utterly dispensed with the usual learned scaffolding of footnotes and appendices, preferring to believe that Hearne is more than capable of telling his own tale. I have taken what may well be considered outrageous liberties with the original text, by rearranging and abridging the material, and by considerable modification of the eighteenth-century syntax, punctuation, phraseology and spelling, in order to remove some of the impediments which the years have placed between the reader and the author.

Throughout my task I have been guided by the conviction that Hearne never intended his story to be hidden away under academic winding-clothes until it achieved the holy remoteness of a religious relic; but that on the contrary he *did* intend it to be read by Everyman, for what it is – the chronicle of a magnificent adventure.

FARLEY MOWAT
Palgrave, Ontario,
January, 1958.

Samuel Hearne was born in London, England, in 1745. When he was three years old his father died, and his mother took him to Dorsetshire where she tried to give him a gentleman's education. It did not take. Not even the heavy-handed eighteenth-century schoolmasters could make him display any interest in scholastic studies, and the only thing for which he showed real aptitude was drawing. His mother gave up the attempt and decided to send him into business, but Hearne would have none of that either. He wanted to go to sea, and eventually his mother agreed to let him join the navy.

He was eleven years old when he boarded the flagship of Captain (later Lord) Hood, as a midshipman. Within the year he had taken part in a brisk battle with the French and had been awarded prize money.

When the war ended, and chances of promotion faded, Hearne decided to leave the Royal Navy. In 1766 he took service with the Hudson's Bay Company and in August of that year arrived at Fort Prince of Wales at the mouth of the Churchill River on Hudson Bay. He was employed for the next two years as mate of the sixty-ton sloop Churchill, engaged in trading with the Eskimos on the west shore of the Bay and in the whale fishery at Marble Island. Hearne did well with the Company, but he grew restive at the Fort and began to agitate for a commission which would allow him greater scope for adventure and achievement. He found both, in his journey to the Coppermine River.

One

THE NORTHERN Indians, who range over the immense tract of land lying north and west of the Churchill River, very often brought samples of copper ore to the Hudson's Bay Company's factory at Prince of Wales Fort. Many of the Company people there conjectured that this ore was found not far from the settlements; and as the Indians informed them that the mines were not very distant from a large river, it was supposed that this river must empty itself into Hudson's Bay.

Although the first accounts of this grand river, together with samples of the copper, were brought to the Company's factory at Churchill River immediately after its establishment in 1715, it does not appear that an attempt was made to discover the river or the mines until 1719, when the Company fitted out the ship *Albany Frigate* and the sloop *Discovery* to investigate the matter. Command of this expedition was given to James Knight, who had made the first settlement at Churchill River.

The disadvantage of having nothing to direct him but the slender and imperfect accounts he had from the Indians (who were then but little known or understood), together with his advanced age of nearly eighty years, by no means discouraged this bold adventurer. He was in fact so certain of success that he took with him some large iron-bound chests to hold gold dust and other valuables which he fondly believed were to be found in those parts.

Mr. Knight soon put out from England, and when his ships did not return that year as was expected, it was judged that they had wintered in Hudson's Bay. However, when neither ship nor sloop returned to England in the year 1720, the Company grew alarmed, and the sloop *Whalebone*, John Scroggs, Master, was sent in search of them. But the north-west coast of Hudson's Bay was little known in those days. Mr. Scroggs found himself greatly embarrassed with shoals and rocks, and returned to Prince of Wales Fort without making any certain discovery as to the fate of the missing vessels.

Some people thereupon conjectured that Mr. Knight had found a North West Passage and had gone through it into the South Sea by way of California.

In 1767 the Company was carrying on a whale fishery at Marble Island. One of the boats, on the lookout for whales, had occasion to row close to the island, and the crew discovered a new harbour near the eastern end. At the head of this harbour they found guns, anchors, cables, bricks, a smith's anvil, and many other articles which the hand of time had not defaced. The remains of a house, though pulled to pieces by the Eskimos in search of wood and nails, was also plain to see, as were the hulls of a ship and sloop which lay sunk in five fathoms in the harbour. So there was no doubt that Mr. Knight and all his company were lost on that inhospitable island where neither stick nor stump was to be seen, and which lies sixteen miles from the mainland, itself little better than a jumble of barren hills and rocks.

In the summer of 1769 we saw several Eskimos at the new harbour, and perceiving that one or two of them were greatly advanced in years our curiosity was excited to ask them some questions. In this we were assisted by an Eskimo who was then in the Company's service as a linguist, and annually sailed in one of our vessels.

They told us that when Mr. Knight's vessels reached

Marble Island it was very late in the fall, and the larger of them received much damage while getting into harbour. The English, numbering about fifty, then began to build a house. As soon as the ice permitted in the summer of 1720, the Eskimos paid them another visit, by which time their number was greatly reduced, and those that were living seemed very unhealthy.

Sickness and famine occasioned such havoc among the English that by the beginning of the second winter their numbers were reduced to twenty. The Eskimos took up their abode on the opposite side of the harbour and frequently supplied them with such provisions as they had, which chiefly consisted of whale's blubber and seal's flesh, and oil. With the advance of spring the Eskimos went back to the mainland, and on their next visit in the summer of 1721 they found only five Englishmen still alive. These were in such distress for provisions that they eagerly ate the seal's flesh and whale's blubber quite raw, as they purchased it from the natives.

The food disordered them so much that three of them died in a few days and the other two, though very weak, made shift to bury them. Those two survived many days after the rest, and frequently went to the top of an adjacent rock, and earnestly looked to the south and east as if in expectation of some vessels coming to their relief. After continuing there a considerable time, and nothing appearing in sight, they sat down close together and wept bitterly. At length one of the two died, and the other's strength was so far exhausted that he fell down and died also, in attempting to dig a grave for his companion.

Thus we heard how the first attempt to find the copper mines had ended.

Some Northern Indians who came to trade at Prince of Wales Fort brought further accounts of the grand river in the spring of 1768, together with several pieces of copper. This determined Mr. Moses Norton, who was then Governor at the Fort, to go to England and represent to the Company that here was an affair worthy of their attention. In consequence, the Committee resolved to send an intelligent person by land to observe the longitude and latitude of the river's mouth, and to make a chart of the country he might walk through, with such remarks as occurred to him during the journey. I was pitched on as a proper person to conduct the expedition, and in the summer of 1769, while I was in my twenty-fourth year, the Company requested me to undertake it.

I did not hesitate to comply. In the following November, when some Northern Indians came to trade, Mr. Norton engaged some of them as my guides, though none had been at the Coppermine River. I was fitted out with ammunition and everything thought necessary to serve two years. I was to be accompanied by two white servants of the Company, two of the Home Guard (Cree Indians employed by the Company at the southern factories), and a sufficient number of Northern Indians to carry my baggage.

Having made every necessary arrangement for my departure on the 6th of November, I took leave of the Governor and my other friends at Prince of Wales Fort and began my journey, under the salute of seven cannon.

On the 9th, after we had crossed Seal River, I asked the leader of the Northern Indians, Captain Chawchinahaw, how long it would take to reach the main woods, for we were then travelling north-westward on the inhospitable barren ground. He assured me that it would only be four or five days, which news put me and my companions in good spirits. But his accounts were so far from being true that, after we had walked ten days, no signs of woods were to be seen in the direction we were steering, though we had often seen the loom of woods to the south-west.

The cold being now very intense, and our small stock of English provisions all expended, and not the least thing to be got on the bleak hills over which we had been walking, the Indians were at last forced to strike more to the westward until, on the 19th, we arrived at some small patches of scrubby woods where we killed a few partridges.

On the 21st, the Indian men went a-hunting while the women cut holes in the ice and caught a few fish from a small lake nearby. At night the men returned with three caribou, or deer, as they are more usually called, which were very acceptable; but our numbers being great, and the Indians having such enormous stomachs, very little was left but fragments after two or three good meals.

Having repaired the sledges and snowshoes we again proceeded in a north-westerly direction and frequently saw the tracks of deer and many musk-oxen, but were not fortunate enough to kill any. A few partridges were all we could get to live on and they were so scarce as to amount to only half a bird a day for each man.

It was now clear that Captain Chawchinahaw had not the welfare of the expedition at heart. He constantly painted the difficulties in the worst colours and took every method to dishearten me, while several times hinting at his desire to return to the Factory. When he found that I was still determined to proceed he took more direct methods, one of which was to cease contributing to our support.

Finding that even this treatment was not likely to complete his design, and that we could not be starved into compliance, he persuaded many of the Northern Indians to desert, taking with them several bags of ammunition and other useful articles. He then explained to me that it would not be prudent to continue farther, and that he and all the rest of his people intended to strike off another way to rejoin their families. He gave me instructions as to the route home, and departed to the southwest, making the woods ring with his laughter as he went, and leaving us to consider our unhappy situation. We were then nearly two hundred miles from Prince of Wales Fort, with our strength and spirits greatly reduced by hunger and fatigue.

Our situation did not permit of much time for reflection. Throwing away some bags of shot and powder, we set off for home. In the course of the day's walk we were fortunate enough to kill several partridges, which made the first meal we had had in several days, and on the 11th of December we arrived back at Prince of Wales Fort, to my own great mortification and to the surprise of the Governor. Thus ended my first attempt to find the grand river of the copper mines.

Two

DURING my absence, several Northern Indians had arrived at the Factory in great distress from hunger. One of these, named Conneequese, said that he had once been very near the river that I sought, and accordingly Mr. Norton engaged him with two other Northern Indians to accompany me on a second attempt.

To avoid all encumbrances as much as possible, Mr. Norton ruled that we would take no women, although he well knew we could not do without their assistance for hauling our baggage, dressing skins for clothing, pitching camp, getting wood, and for other purposes.

On my part I would permit no European to go with me, for on the previous journey the Indians had paid so little heed to Isbester and Merriman, my two English companions, that I was determined to leave them behind. Isbester was very desirous to accompany me again, but Merriman was quite sick of such excursions, and seemed to be very thankful that he had once more arrived in safety amongst his friends.

I was again fitted out with a large supply of ammunition and as many other useful articles as we could take, together with a small sample of light trading goods intended as presents to the Indians we might meet.

On the 23rd of February, 1770, I began my second journey, accompanied by three of the Northern Indians and two of our Home Guard Southerners. The snow was by then so deep on the ramparts of the Fort that few of the cannon were to be seen; otherwise the Governor would have saluted my departure as before. However, as these honours could not possibly have been of service to me, I readily relinquished them.

The first part of our course was much the same as previously, but when we reached Seal River, we followed its course westward, instead of striking across it into the barren grounds.

The winter weather was so remarkably boisterous and changeable that we were frequently obliged to stay two or three nights in the same camp. To make up for this inconvenience the deer were so plentiful, for the first eight or ten days, that the Indians killed all we needed; but we were so heavily laden that we could not possibly take much of the meat with us. This I soon perceived to be a great evil which exposed us – in the event of not killing anything for three or four days – to a severe want of provisions. However, we seldom went to bed entirely supperless until the 8th of March, when we could not produce a single thing to eat, not even a partridge. This being the case, we prepared some hooks and lines with which to angle for fish through the ice of Sheethanee Lake, near which we had encamped.

On the morning of the 9th, we moved our tent some five miles westward to a part of the lake which seemed more commodious for fishing. As soon as we arrived some of our people were employed cutting holes in the ice, while others pitched the tent and gathered firewood. Then, since it was still early in the morning, some of the men went hunting, while the rest fished through the ice. The hunters were successful in catching a porcupine which, with several trout caught in the lake, afforded a plentiful supper and even left something over for breakfast.

Fishing through the ice requires the cutting of a hole one or two feet in diameter, through which the hook is lowered. The line must, however, be kept in motion to prevent the water from freezing, as it does very quickly if allowed to remain undisturbed. The motion is also found to be a great allurement to the fish in these parts, for they will take a bait which is in motion much sooner than one that is at rest.

There are several absurd superstitions attached to the way the Northern Indians angle. When they bait a hook, a composition of four to six articles, by way of a charm, is concealed under the bait, which itself is always sewed to the hook. In fact the only bait they use is a composition of charms enclosed in a bit of fish skin and shaped in some measure to resemble a small fish. The charms used are bits of beaver's tail and fat, otter's vents and teeth, musk-rat's guts and tails, loon's vents, squirrel's testicles, the curdled milk from the stomach of a suckling fawn, human hair, and numberless other articles.

Every master of a family, and almost every other person, has a small bundle of such trash which they always carry with them, summer and winter. Without some of these articles few of them could be prevailed upon to put a hook in water, being persuaded that they might as well sit in their tents as angle without such assistance.

For the succeeding ten days we caught fish enough to survive, but on the 19th, catching nothing, we moved our camp eight miles farther to the westward on this same lake, and that night caught several fine pike. The following day we moved again, this time to the river which flows into Sheethanee from Negassa Lake. Here we set four nets and, in the course of the day, caught many fine fish, particularly pike, trout and tittymeg or whitefish.

In order to set a net under the ice, the Indians first stretch it out full length near where it is to be set; then they cut a series of holes in the ice at a distance of ten or twelve feet apart, along the whole length of the net. A line is then passed under the ice by means of a long, light pole, which can reach from one hole to the next. The net is tied to the end of the line and is drawn under. Finally the free end of the line is brought back over the ice, and tied to the other end of the net so that line and net together form an unbroken circlet.

In order to search such a net, the two end holes are broken open, the line is veered away by one person and the net hauled from under the ice by another.

When these people make a fishing net, which is always composed of small thongs cut from raw deer-skins, they take a number of birds' bills and feet and tie them to the head and foot ropes of the net. At the four corners they generally fasten some of the toes and jaws of otters. The birds chosen are usually the laughing goose, wavey, gulls, and loons, and unless the parts of some or all of these are fastened to the net, the Indians will not even put it in the water.

The first fish of whatever species caught must be broiled whole before the fire, and the flesh carefully removed from the bones without dislocating one joint. Afterwards the bones are laid in the fire and burnt.

When they fish in rivers or narrow channels that join two lakes, they could frequently – by tying several nets together – cover the whole width of the channel and intercept every sizable fish that passed. Instead of doing this they scatter the individual nets at a considerable distance from one another, in the belief that, if they were kept close, one net would be jealous of its neighbour and none of them would catch a single fish.

Now as this place where we were camped seemed likely to afford us a constant supply of fish, my guide proposed to stay here till the geese began to fly. "The weather," he said, "is too cold to walk on the barren grounds, and, since the woods hereabouts trend to the west, if we continued to stay within them as we travelled, our course would not be better than west-south-west, which would be going far out of our way. However, if we remain here until the weather permits us to walk due north, we shall get on our way very quickly."

These reasons appeared judicious, and as the plan

seemed likely to be attended by little trouble, it met with my entire approbation. That being the case, we took additional pains in building our tent, and made it as commodious as conditions would allow.

To pitch an Indian tent in winter one must first find a level place by testing through the snow with a stick. The snow must then be cleared away in a circular space down to the moss and, when it is proposed to remain more than a night or two, the moss is also removed as it is very liable to catch fire when dry, and thus occasion much trouble to the inhabitants.

A number of poles are then procured. If one of these should not happen to be conveniently forked, two of them are tied near the top and then raised erect with their butts extending as wide as the diameter of the tent. The other poles are then set around at equal distances from one another, so that their lower ends form a complete circle. The covering is fastened to a light stick which is raised up against the framework in such a manner that, when the covering is wrapped around, the door will always be to leeward. This however, only holds good for travel camps. If the tent is to stand for any length of time, the door will always face the south.

The covering, or tent-cloth, is made of thin moose leather, and in shape it resembles an open fan, so that when the larger curve encloses the bottom of the framework, the smaller is sufficient to cover the top, leaving a hole which is designed to serve as chimney and window.

The fire is built on the ground in the centre of the tent, and the remainder of the floor is covered with small pine branches which serve as beds and seats. Pine tops and branches are also laid around the bottom of the tent on the outside, and the covering is staked down over them, then snow is packed part way up the outer walls to exclude the external air. This type of tent is made by the Southern Indians, and was the kind furnished me for my journey. As for the Northern Indians, their tents are of different materials and shape, as shall be described hereafter.

The situation of our camp was truly pleasant, being on a small elevated point which commanded an extensive prospect over a large lake, the shores of which abounded in pine, larch, birch, and poplar, beautifully contrasted with high hills which showed their snowy summits above the tallest trees.

The remaining part of March passed without occurrence worth relating. Our nets provided us with sufficient food and our Indians had too much philosophy about them to give themselves such additional trouble as even to look for a partridge with which to vary their diet. I brought up my journal, observed the latitude of this place with my quadrant, and filled up my chart. I also built some traps and caught a few marten. These marten were trapped by means of a few logs so arranged that when the animal attempted to take away the bait he pulled down a small post that supported the weight of the logs. I also snared some partridges by making little hedges projecting at right angles from a small island, leaving openings provided with snares, for the partridges to pass through.

On the first of April, to our great surprise, the nets did not yield a single fish. We then went out to angle, but could not procure a fish the whole day. This sudden change of circumstance alarmed one of my companions so much that he even began to think of resuming the use of his gun, after having laid it by for near a month.

In the morning, Conneequese went hunting while the rest attended the hooks and nets, but with such bad success that we could not procure enough fish to serve two men for supper.

My guide, who was a steady man, closely pursued the hunting, seldom returning to the tent till after dark, but without success for several days. On the 10th he continued away longer than usual. We lay down to sleep, having had but little refreshment for three days, except a pipe of tobacco and a draught of water. About midnight, to our great joy, our hunter arrived home, bringing the blood, and fragments, of two deer that he had killed. In an instant we were busy cooking a large kettle of broth made with the blood and some scraps of fat and meat shreds boiled with it. This might be reckoned a dainty dish at any time, but was particularly so in our present famished state.

Several days were now spent in feasting and gluttony, during which the Indians killed five more deer and three fine beavers. The flesh of the deer might, with frugality, have served the six of us for some time, but my companions feasted day and night while the meat lasted, and were so indolent and unthinking as not to attend the nets during this time, so that many fine fish that had been entangled were entirely spoiled. Consequently after about fourteen days we were nearly in as great distress for provisions as ever.

On the 24th of April a great body of Indians was seen approaching from the south-west. On their arrival we discovered them to be the wives and families of Northern Indians who were gone to Prince of Wales Fort. These people were bound toward the barren ground to await the return of their husbands and relations.

My guide determined to move to the barren ground also, so we took down our tent on the morning of the 27th and proceeded eastward in company with some of the newcomers. It was the 13th of May before we could procure any of the birds we saw flying north. On that day the Indians killed two swans and three geese. These somewhat alleviated our distress, which was very great, for we had found no other subsistence for five or six days other than a few old cranberries gathered from the dry ridges where the snow had melted. The Northern Indians who had joined us had stocks of dried meat by them, but though they secretly provided for our Northern guides, they gave me and my Southern Indians not the least supply.

However, by the 19th of May the geese, swans and ducks were in such numbers that we killed as many as we needed to recruit our spirits after such a long fast.

We proceeded on toward the barren ground, with my crew augmented to twelve persons by the addition of one of my guide's wives, and five others whom I engaged to assist in carrying our luggage when the hauling season ended, as it soon would. Already the thaws had rendered travelling in the woods impracticable, so we continued our eastward course on Seal River until we came to a smaller river and a string of lakes which tended to the north.

Game of all kinds was plentiful as we walked northward on the ice, until the first of June when we arrived at a place called Beralzone. On the way one of my companions had the misfortune to shatter his hand by the bursting of his gun, but I bound up the wound and, with the assistance of some Turlington's Drops, yellow basilicon, etc., I soon restored the use of his hand so that in a very short time he seemed to be out of danger.

We stopped a few days at Beralzone to dry some venison and some geese beside a fire, for we were soon to be clear of the woods where fuel was easy to procure.

By the 6th, the thaws were so general and the snows so melted that our snowshoes were attended by more trouble than service, so we cast them away. The sledges still proved useful, particularly in crossing lakes and ponds on the ice; but on the 10th, that mode of travel growing dangerous, we determined to throw away the sledges and everyone had to take a load on his back.

This I found to be hard work, since my luggage consisted of the following articles: the quadrant and its stand, a trunk containing books and papers, a land compass, and a large bag containing all my wearing apparel; also a hatchet, knives, and files, besides several small articles intended for presents to the natives. The awkwardness of my load, and its weight, combined with the excessive heat during the day, rendered walking the most laborious task

I had ever encountered. The badness of the road and the coarseness of our lodging – on account of the present want of tents – exposed us to the utmost severity of the weather and greatly increased our hardships.

The tent I had brought with us was too large for the barren grounds where no poles are to be had, and so we had cut it up for moccasins, each person carrying his own share. My guide had never made us acquainted with the methods of pitching a tent in the barrens, but he had cunningly procured a set of small, portable poles for himself and his wife. When our tent was divided, he made shift to get a piece big enough to serve him as a complete little tent, and he never asked either me or my Southern Indians to put our heads inside of it.

We also experienced real distress for want of victuals. What little we got we were forced to consume raw, for lack of fuel; and raw fish, particularly, was little relished by either my Southern companions or myself.

Notwithstanding these complicated hardships, we continued in perfect health and in good spirits, and my guide, though a perfect niggard of his provisions, gave us the strongest assurances of soon arriving at a plentiful country where we would not only find a sure supply of provisions, but would meet other Indians who would probably be willing to carry part of our luggage. This gave us much consolation, for the weight of our luggage was so great that we could scarcely carry two days' provisions on top of it, which was the chief reason of our being so frequently in want.

From the 20th to the 23rd of June, we walked nearly twenty miles a day without any subsistence other than a pipe of tobacco and a drink of water when we pleased. Early on the 23rd we saw three musk-oxen, and the Indians soon killed them. But to our great mortification it rained before we got them skinned, and the moss could not be made to burn to make a fire. This was poor comfort for people who had not broken their fast for three or four days. Necessity, however, has no law, even though the raw flesh of musk-oxen is not only coarse and tough, but smells and tastes most disagreeably of musk.

The weather remained so bad, with rain, snow, and sleet, that by the time we were again able to make a fire of moss, we had eaten the amount of one musk-ox quite raw.

I must confess that now my spirits began to fail me a little. Indeed our other misfortunes were greatly aggravated by the weather, which was cold and so very wet that for three days and nights I had not one dry thread on me. But when the fine weather returned, and we had dried our clothing by a fire of moss, I endeavoured, like a sailor after a storm, to forget past misfortunes; for it seemed that things would now go forward in the old channel, even though it was an indifferent one indeed.

None of our wants, except thirst, are so distressing as hunger, and in wandering situations the hardship is greatly aggravated by the uncertainty as to its duration. The labour and fatigue we must necessarily undergo in seeking to relieve the hunger, and the disappointments which too frequently frustrate our attempts, not only enfeeble the body but depress the spirit. Besides, for want of action, the stomach so far loses its digestive powers that after long fasting it resumes its office only with pain and reluctance. During my journeys I have all too frequently experienced these dreadful effects, and more than once have been reduced to such a low state that, when Providence threw something my way, my stomach was scarcely able to retain more than two or three ounces without producing the most oppressive pains.

Another disagreeable circumstance of long fasting is the extreme difficulty and pain attending the natural evacuation for the first time after eating; it is so dreadful that none but those who have experienced it can have an adequate idea of its effect.

Our journey to this point had been either feast or famine. Sometimes we had too much, seldom just enough, frequently too little, and often none at all. We often fasted two days and nights; twice, three days, and once, upward of seven days, during which we tasted not a mouthful of anything except a few cranberries, scraps of old leather, and burnt bones. On these pressing occasions I have often seen the Indians examining their wardrobes and considering what part could best be spared; sometimes a piece of an old, half-rotten deer skin, and at others a pair of old moccasins, were sacrificed to alleviate extreme hunger. However, these are no more than common occurrences in the Indians' life, in which they are sometimes even driven to the necessity of eating one another.

Although it is well known that they are never guilty of such horrid repasts except when they are driven to it, yet those who have eaten human flesh are shunned and universally detested by all that know them. I have seen several of these poor wretches and, though they were much esteemed persons before hunger drove them to this act, yet afterwards they were so despised that a smile never graced their faces. Deep melancholy was seated on their brows, and their eyes seemed to say: "Why do you despise me for my misfortune? The period is probably not far distant when you too may be driven to the like necessity."

Three

W<small>E CONTINUED</small> in the place where we had killed the musk-oxen for a day or two, both to refresh ourselves and to dry a little meat, as it thereby becomes more portable and also is always ready for use.

The preparation of meat in this manner is very simple, requiring no further operation than cutting the lean part of the animal into thin slices and drying it in the sun, or before a slow fire. It may then, if one wishes, be pounded between two stones until it is reduced to a coarse powder, when it is even more compact to carry.

On the 26th of June we again proceeded northward and on the 30th arrived at a river called Cathawhachaga, which empties itself into a very large lake called Yathkyed Whoie, or White Snow Lake.

Here we found several tents of Indians who were employed spearing deer from their canoes, as these animals crossed the river on their journey to the north. Here also we met a Northern Indian leader or "Captain" called Keelshies who, with a small band, was bound to Prince of Wales Fort with furs.

When Keelshies was made acquainted with the intent of my journey he volunteered to bring me anything from the Fort that we were likely to need, and he promised to join us again, at a place appointed by my guide, when winter set in. As we were somewhat short of tobacco, powder, shot, and other articles for trade, I determined to send a letter to the Governor, and although we were more than three hundred miles northwest of the Fort, I asked for the articles I needed to be sent on to me by the hand of Captain Keelshies.

The ceremonies which pass when two parties of Northern Indians meet are very curious. After advancing to within twenty yards of each other, both parties make a full halt and sit or lie on the ground, without speaking, for some minutes. At length an elderly man, if one be in the company, breaks the silence by acquainting the other party with every misfortune that has befallen him and his comrades from the time they last saw or heard of the other group. This lament includes also the deaths and calamities that have befallen other Indians during the same period, as far as the particulars are known to the orator.

When the first has finished, another ancient orator of the other party relates all the bad news that has come to *his* knowledge. If this exchange contains news which in the least affects any of those present, it is not long before some of them begin to sigh and sob, and then break into loud cries. They are generally accompanied in this by most of the grown persons of both sexes, and it is not uncommon to see them all – men, women and children – united in one universal howl. In fact I never remember seeing one of these crying matches, as I called them, in which the greatest part of the company did not assist, although some of them had no reason for it, except seeing their companions do the same.

When the first transports of grief have subsided, the two parties advance and mix with one another, the men with the men, and the women with the women. If they have any tobacco, the pipes are passed around pretty freely, and the conversation becomes general. As they have already disposed of all the bad news, they have nothing left but good to talk about, which has such a predominance over the former that smiles and cheerfulness are soon to be seen on every face. If they happen not to be in want, the exchange of small presents of provisions, ammunition and other articles often takes place – sometimes as a gift, but more frequently by way of seeing whether they cannot elicit a greater present in return.

These people have but few diversions. The chief is shooting at a mark with bows and arrows. Another sport, called *holl*, in some measure resembles quoits, only it is played with clubs sharpened on one end.

They also amuse themselves at times with dancing, which is always performed in the night. Yet it is remarkable that these people, though a distinct nation, have never adopted any mode of dancing of their own, so that on the few occasions when anything of this kind is attempted, they endeavour to imitate either the Dog-ribbed or the Southern Indians.

The Dog-ribbed method is not very difficult, as it only consists in lifting the feet alternately in a very quick succession, and as high as possible, without moving the body. At the same time the hands are clenched and held close to the breast, while the head is inclined forward. They always dance quite naked except for the breech clout, and at times even this is thrown off. The dancers, who seldom exceed three or four at a time, stand close to the music which, by straining a point, may be called both vocal and instrumental – though both are sufficiently humble. The former is only a frequent repetition of the words *hee, hee, hee, ho, ho, ho,* etc., which by repetition, and different emphasis, and the raising and lowering of the voice, produces something like a tune. The singing is accompanied by a drum or tabor, and sometimes by a kind of rattle made with a piece of dried buffalo-skin shaped like an oil flask, into which they put some pebbles or shot.

This mode of dancing naked is performed only by the men. When the women are ordered to dance, they do so outside the tent, to music which is played within it. Though their dancing is perfectly decent, it has still less meaning and action than that of the men. A whole heap of them crowd together in a line and simply shuffle themselves a little from right to left and back again, without lifting their feet from the ground. When the music stops they all give a little bend, like an awkward curtsy, and pronounce in a shrill tone: *h-e-e-e h-o-o-o!*

Besides these diversions they have a simple indoor gambling game. They take a bit of wood, a button, or other small thing, and after shifting it from hand to hand several times, ask their antagonist which hand it is in. Each of the two persons engaged has a number of small chips of wood, and when one of the players guesses right, he takes a piece of wood from his opponent's pile. He that first gets all the sticks is said to win the stake, which is generally a single load of powder, an arrow, or some other thing of inconsiderable value.

As we had not any canoes with us we were obliged to get ferried across the Cathawhachaga River by the strange Indians we had met there. When we had reached the north bank, my guide proposed that we halt for a time and dry and pound some deer meat to take with us. I readily consented, and we also set our nets and caught a quantity of fish. However, the numbers of deer crossing the river were scarcely sufficient to our daily needs, so that on the 6th of July we were forced to set out again with no more victuals than would furnish us a supper.

On preparing to leave, my guide informed me that a canoe would be absolutely necessary to cross some unfordable rivers ahead of us, and this induced me to purchase one from the strange Indians at the easy rate of a knife, the full value of which did not exceed a penny.

The canoes made by these people were extremely small, and scarce able to carry two men, one of whom had to lie full length on the bottom. Nevertheless this additional piece of luggage obliged me to engage another Indian; and we were lucky enough to get a poor, forlorn fellow who was used to the office, never having been in a much better state than that of a beast of burthen.

Thus provided, we left Cathawhachaga and continued our course over open rocky plains toward the north and west. On the 17th we saw many musk-oxen, seven of which the Indians killed, and we halted a day or two to dry and pound some of the meat. Nevertheless when we proceeded we left behind us a great quantity of meat which we could neither eat nor carry.

On the 22nd we met several strange Indians whom we joined in pursuit of the deer, which had now become so plentiful that we got sufficient every day for our support, and too frequently killed several merely for the tongues, marrow and fat.

We had by now reached a great watery plain lying about four hundred and fifty miles to the north-west of Prince of Wales Fort, and my guide seemed to hesitate about proceeding farther. Instead he kept pitching our camp back and forth in company with the strange Indians who were only engaged in following the roving deer, wherever these might choose to lead. On my asking him the reason for his action, he answered that the year was too far advanced to admit of reaching the Coppermine River that summer, and we would be better served to winter with the Indians we had met, in their country to the south, and to proceed the following summer. As I could not pretend to contradict him, I was reconciled to his proposal. Accordingly we kept moving with the other Indians, who became daily more numerous until by the 30th of July we had in all about seventy tents, which contained at least six hundred persons. Indeed our encampment at night had the appearance of a small town, and in the morning, when we began to move, the whole country seemed to be alive with men, women, children, and dogs which carried packs upon their backs.

It may not be amiss to give some description of the people with whom I was now living. These Northern Indians are, in general, above middle size, being well-proportioned, strong and robust. Their complexion is somewhat of a copper cast, and their hair is black and straight. Few of the men have any beard, and those who do, have no other method of eradicating it than of pulling it out between their fingers and the edge of a blunt knife. Neither sex have any hair under their armpits, and very little on any other part of their body, particularly the women; but on the place where Nature plants the hair, I have never known them attempt to eradicate it.

Their features are peculiar, and different from any other tribe in those parts; for they have low foreheads, small eyes, high cheek-bones, Roman noses and, in general, long broad chins. Their skins are soft, smooth and polished, and when they are dressed in clean clothing they are as free from an offensive smell as any of the human race.

Every tribe of Northern Indians, as well as the Copper and Dog-ribbed Indians, have three or four parallel black strokes marked on each cheek, which is performed by entering a needle or awl under the skin and immediately rubbing powdered charcoal into the wound.

Their dispositions are in general morose and covetous, and they are forever pleading poverty, even among themselves. When any real distressed objects present themselves at the Company's factory, they are always relieved with victuals, clothes, medicines, and every other necessity, gratis; and in return they instruct every one of their countrymen how to behave, in order to obtain the same charity. I know of no people that have more command of their passions on such occasions; in this respect the women exceed the men, and I can affirm with truth I have seen some of them with one side of the face bathed in tears, while the other has exhibited a significant smile.

They differ so much from the rest of mankind that harsh, uncourteous usage seems to agree better with the generality of them, particularly the lower class, than mild treatment. If the least respect is shown them it makes them insolent, and though some of their leaders may be exempt from this characteristic, yet there are few even of them who have sense enough to set a proper value on favours and indulgences.

Though the ground over which we were now travelling was entirely barren, and destitute of every kind of herbage except dwarf shrubs and moss, yet the deer were so numerous that the Indians not only killed as many as were sufficient for our large numbers, but often killed merely for the skins, the marrow, etc., and left the carcasses to rot or to be devoured by the wolves and foxes.

We moved westward until we crossed the Dubawnt River which, with its immense lake, was fresh, proving that we had not yet come near the northern coast.

Here we had recourse to our small canoe. This method of ferrying a party over a river, while it is tedious because of the many trips to and fro, is the most expeditious way these poor people can contrive. They are sometimes obliged to carry their canoes two hundred miles on their backs without having occasion to make use of them, and if they were not so small and portable it would be impossible for one man to carry them.

The weather remained fair, and we walked but short days' journeys, and the deer remained plentiful, so that all things went smoothly until the 8th of August.

I intended to have a little sport with the deer that day, and knowing that one of my Northern Indians had a lighter pack than mine, I gave him the quadrant and stand to carry; which he took without seeming ill-will. Having thus eased myself, I set out with my Southern Indians, and after walking eight miles I saw, from the top of a high hill, a very great number of deer feeding in a neighbouring valley. My companions and I laid down our gear and pursued our hunting; but when we returned to the hill that evening I found that only part of the Northern Indians had arrived, and the one who carried the quadrant, and our powder, was not amongst them.

The evening being far advanced, we could not go in search of him till morning. The Southern Indians and myself were very uneasy, fearing that we had lost the powder which was to provide us with food and raiment for the remainder of the journey. The uncourteous behaviour of the Northern Indians then in our company gave me little hope of getting any assistance from them now that I no longer had the wherewithal to reward them for their trouble. In fact, during the whole time I had been with them, not one had offered to give me the least morsel of victuals without asking for something, three times the value, in exchange.

So inconsiderate were these people that, wherever they met me, they always expected that I had a great assortment of goods to trade, as if indeed I had brought the Company's warehouse with me. When they found I had nothing much to spare, they pronounced me a "poor servant, noways like the Governor" who, they said, always gave them something useful. It is scarce possible to conceive of any people so wanting in understanding as to think I was making this fatiguing journey with the sole intent of bringing them everything of which they stood in need.

This unaccountable behaviour of the Indians occasioned much serious reflection on my part, as it showed plainly how little I had to expect if, by some accident, I should have to depend on them for support. As I laid me down to rest, after losing the quadrant and powder, sleep was a stranger to me for a long time, and I even repeated some beautiful lines by Dr. Young a hundred times without gaining any slumber by it.

After this melancholy night, I got up at daybreak and, with the two Southern Indians, set out in search of the deserter. Many hours elapsed in a fruitless quest, as we could not discover a single track in the direction he was supposed to have taken.

The day being almost spent, with no appearance of success, I at last proposed returning to the place where I had given him the quadrant, in the hopes of finding some track in the moss which would tell us which way he had gone. On our arrival at the place we found that he had struck off toward a little river, and there, to our great joy, we found the quadrant and the bag of powder lying on the top of a stone, though not a human being was in sight.

On examining the bag we discovered that part of the powder had been taken, but notwithstanding this considerable loss we returned with light hearts to where we had left our guide, only to find that he and all the other Indians were gone from there. They had, however, been so considerate as to set up marks to direct our course, and a little after ten o'clock at night we came up with them. After a plentiful supper, the first morsel we had touched that day, we retired to rest, which I at least enjoyed with better success than the preceding night.

I might not have slept so sound had I been aware of what was in store for me; for on the 12th of August, when I had set the quadrant on its stand and was eating my dinner, to my great mortification a sudden gust of wind blew the quadrant down. The ground was stony, and the bubble, vernier and sight-vane were broken to pieces, rendering the instrument of no further use.

In consequence of this bitter misfortune, which made it impossible for me to obtain any further latitudes, I was forced to the hard resolve of returning once again to the Fort, even though I was then almost five hundred miles west-north-west of Churchill River, and had thought myself to be well advanced toward the goal I sought.

Four

ON THE DAY after I had the misfortune to break my quadrant, several Indians joined us from the northward, and some of them plundered me and my companions of every useful article we had, among which was my gun; but it not being in my power to recover what had been taken, we were obliged to rest contented.

Nothing could exceed the cool deliberation of these villains. A committee of them entered my tent (for we had now contrived to make ourselves a shelter, using some walking-sticks with a blanket thrown over them) and the ringleader sat himself on my left hand. They first begged me to lend them my *skipertogan* (a small bag containing flint and steel, pipe, tobacco, and some touch-wood for making a fire), and after smoking two or three pipes they asked for several articles which I had not. One of them then put his hand on my baggage and in an instant he and his five companions had all my treasures spread on the ground. One took one thing, and one another, until nothing was left but the empty bag. On my earnest request, they gave back a knife, an awl and a needle, though not without making me understand that I ought to look upon this as a great favour.

Finding them possessed of so much generosity, I ventured to solicit them for my razors but, thinking that one would suffice to shave me during the passage home, they made no scruple of keeping the other one – luckily they chose the worst. To complete their generosity, they permitted me to take as much soap as I would need to shave and wash myself until I reached the Fort.

They were somewhat more cautious in plundering my Southern Indians. Such an outrage might have occasioned a war between the two nations, whereas they had nothing of that kind to dread from the English. However, they managed, by threats, to talk the Home Guard out of all they had, so they were as clean swept as myself except for their guns, some ammunition, an old hatchet, an ice-chisel and a file.

My guide, being a man of little note, was quite unable to protect us and was obliged to submit to the same outrage as ourselves. He assumed a great air of generosity, though the fact was that he gave freely of what was not in his power to retain.

Early in the morning of the 19th of August we set out on our return journey, accompanied by some Northern Indians who were bound to the Fort with furs. I had fortunately recovered my gun, since the Indian who took it had no powder or shot and it was therefore of no value to him. Since everything else was taken from me, I found that my load was now so light that this part of the journey was the easiest and most pleasant of any I had experienced; particularly as the deer were plentiful, and the weather fine.

We rounded the bottom of Dubawnt Lake, which is vast enough to be an inland sea, and then proceeded in a south-easterly direction. Frequently we met other Indians, so that scarcely a day passed without our seeing several smokes made by strangers. Many of these joined our party, having furs to trade which they had gathered to the westward during the previous winter.

By the end of August the deer's hair was of the proper length for the making of clothing, so that all of us were soon busied gathering hides against our winter needs. Since it requires the prime parts of eight to eleven deer-skins to make a suit, it must be imagined that the addition to our burdens was very considerable.

Yet after I had carried my load of hides for many weeks, it proved of no service, for we had not any women properly belonging to our party, and consequently no one to dress the skins. The other Indians were so uncivil that they would neither allow their women to dress the skins nor exchange them for others of an inferior quality already dressed. I never saw a people with so little humanity, for though they seem to have a great affection for their wives and children, yet they will laugh at, and ridicule, the distress of every other person who is not directly related to them.

As the fall advanced we began to feel the cold very severely, for want of proper clothing. My guide was exempted from this inconvenience, having procured a good warm suit of furs and, as one of his wives was with him, he was provided with a tent and every other necessity. But the old fellow was so far from interesting himself in our behalf that he had, for some time past, entirely withdrawn from our company and did not contribute at all to our support. The deer, however, remained in great plenty and we did not suffer from his neglect in this respect.

Provisions still continued plentiful well into September, which was a singular piece of good fortune, and the only happy circumstance of that part of the journey, for the weather was remarkably bad, and severely cold. We were in a forlorn state as we continued to the southeast until, on the 20th of September, we encountered the famous Captain Matonabbee.

Matonabbee was the son of a Northern Indian, by a slave woman bought from the Southern Indians by Mr. Richard Norton, the father of the present Governor. Mr. Norton himself brought about the match between Matonabbee's father and the slave woman, probably in 1736, and Matonabbee was born soon afterwards.

His father dying while the boy was still young, Mr. Norton then took Matonabbee and, according to Indian custom, adopted him as a son. However, Mr. Norton went to England soon afterwards, and the boy did not experience the same regard from the new Governor. He was therefore taken from the Factory by some of his Northern relations and continued with them until Mr. Ferdinand Jacobs succeeded to the command of Prince of Wales Fort in 1752. Out of regard to old Mr. Norton, who by that time was dead, Mr. Jacobs detained Matonabbee at the Factory for several years.

During the course of his long stay in and near the Fort, he mastered the Southern Indian language perfectly and made some progress in English. He also gained some knowledge of the Christian faith; but he always declared that it was too intricate for his comprehension, and he could by no means be induced to believe in any part of our religion. However, he had so much natural good sense and liberality of sentiment that he would not ridicule any particular sect on account of their religious opinion. He held them all in equal esteem, but was determined that as he came into this world, so he would go out of it – without professing any religion at all. Notwithstanding, I have met few Christians who possessed more good qualities, or fewer bad ones.

It is impossible for any man to have been more punctual in the performance of a promise than he was. His scrupulous adherence to truth and honesty would have done honour to the most enlightened and devout Christian, while his benevolence and universal humanity to all the human race – with but one exception, of which I will speak later – could not have been exceeded by the most illustrious person now on record.

In stature he was above common size, being nearly six feet tall, and except that his neck was rather short he was one of the best proportioned men I ever saw. He was dark, like the other Northern Indians, but his face was not disfigured by the custom of marking the cheeks with three or four black lines. His features were regular and agreeable, yet strong; and in his personality he was most admirable, for he combined the vivacity of a Frenchman and the sincerity of an Englishman with the gravity and nobleness of a Turk.

He was remarkably fond of Spanish wines, though he never drank to excess; and as he would not take spirits, however good they were, he always remained master of himself.

Now, as no man is totally exempt from frailties, it must be imagined that Matonabbee had his share; yet the greatest with which I can charge him is jealousy, and that sometimes carried him beyond the bounds of humanity.

In his early youth he displayed such talents that Mr. Jacobs engaged him as an ambassador and mediator between the Northern and the Athapuscow Indians who, till then, had always been at war with one another. In the pursuit of this task Matonabbee displayed the most brilliant and solid parts, and demonstrated such personal courage and magnanimity as are rarely to be found amongst persons of superior condition and rank.

He had not penetrated far into the country of the Athapuscow Indians (which lies seven or eight hundred miles to the west of Churchill River) before he came to several tents and found, to his great surprise, Captain Keelshies with all his family, held prisoner. Though Matonabbee was young enough to be Keelshies' son, he nevertheless contrived to obtain the release of Keelshies, though that worthy lost all his effects, and his six wives.

After Keelshies and his small party had been permitted to depart, Matonabbee not only held his ground but penetrated into the very heart of the Athapuscow country in order to have a personal conference with all the principal inhabitants.

The farther he advanced, the more occasion he had for bravery. At one Athapuscow camp he and his wife, with a servant boy, were alone amongst sixteen families of the enemy. These Southern Indians, who were always treacherous, seemed to give him a hearty welcome, and invited him to each tent in return for a feast and entertainment, having planned to kill him at the last tent. But he was so perfect a master of their language that he discovered their design and told them that, though he had come without enmity, yet he would sell his life dear enough.

On hearing this, some of them ordered that his gun, snowshoes, and servant should be seized and secured; but Matonabbee sprang from his seat, grasped his gun and leapt outside the tent, telling them that this was the proper place to try and murder him, for then he could see his enemy, and not be shot cowardly through the back.

"I am sure," he said, "of taking two or three of you with me, but if you choose to purchase my life at that price, now is the time. Otherwise let me depart."

They told him he was at liberty, but that he must leave his servant. On hearing this he rushed into the tent and took his servant by force from two men who held him, and only then did he set out on his return to the frontiers of his own country, and from thence to the Factory.

The following year he again visited the Athapuscow country, but this time accompanied by a considerable number of chosen men. Having traversed the whole district with his band, and spoken to all the principal people of the enemy, he thought that peace was at last established. Accordingly Matonabbee's men withdrew into their own lands; but Matonabbee and a few others chose to pass the summer in the Athapuscow country.

As soon as the Southern Indians found the numbers of the Northern Indians so reduced, they dogged and harassed the remainder all summer long, with a view to killing them when they were asleep. Twice they approached so near Matonabbee's tent as fifty yards, but each time he met them as he had done before, saying that he would sell his life dearly enough, and each time the Southern Indians withdrew.

Despite these uncertain receptions, Matonabbee continued to visit the Athapuscow country for several successive years, and finally, by a uniform display of pacific purpose, and by a long train of good offices rendered to the Southern Indians – often in return for treachery and perfidy – he became not only the sole instrument of bringing about a lasting peace, but of establishing a trade and reciprocal interest between the two nations as well.

After performing this great work he was prevailed upon to visit the Coppermine River in company with another famous leader called Idotleaza; and it was from the report of these two men that Mr. Moses Norton was encouraged to obtain permission for an expedition to be sent overland to the Coppermine.

Five

MATONABBEE's courteous behaviour, upon our meeting, struck me greatly. As soon as he was acquainted with our distress he got such skins as we had with us dressed for the Southern Indians, and furnished me with a good warm suit of otter and other skins.

Matonabbee then made a grand feast for me in the Southern Indian style and there was plenty of good eating, and the whole concluded with singing and dancing. My two Southern Indians bore no inconsiderable part, for they were both men of importance in their own lands, though amongst the Northern Indians they were held in no estimation. This is not to be wondered at when we consider that the value of a man amongst these Northern people is proportioned to his hunting ability, and as my Southern Indians showed no great talents in this regard, they received but little respect.

During our conversation, Matonabbee asked me very seriously if I would attempt another journey to the Coppermine River. On my answering in the affirmative, providing I could get better guides than I had hitherto possessed, he said that he would readily engage in this service himself. I assured him that his offer would be very gladly accepted; as I had already experienced every hardship that was likely to accompany a future trial, I was now determined to complete the discovery even at the risk of life itself.

Matonabbee attributed our present misfortunes partly to the misconduct of our guides, but mainly to the insistence of the Governor that we should take no women.

"For," said he, "when all the men are heavy laden, they can neither hunt nor travel any distance. And in case they should meet with some success in hunting, who is to carry the produce of their labour? Women were made for labour. One of them can carry or haul as much as two men. They also pitch our tents, make and mend our clothes, keep us warm at night – and in fact there is no such thing as travelling any considerable distance without their assistance. More than this, women can be maintained at trifling expense, for, as they always cook, the very licking of their fingers in scarce times is sufficient for their sustenance."

After a brief diversion from our route in order to obtain birch-wood for snowshoes and sledges, we rejoined Matonabbee and travelled in concert with him to the south. Deer were plentiful, but the guide had so embezzled our supplies of shot, that we were forced to cut up an ice-chisel into lumps as a substitute for ball. It is, however, rather dangerous firing square lumps of iron out of such weak barrels as are brought into this part of the world for trade.

On the 22nd of November, after parting again from Matonabbee's party in order to speed our way to the Fort, we were caught in a mighty blizzard on the barren plains near the coast. The snow drifted so excessively thick that we could not see our way, and between seven and eight in the evening it grew so bitter cold that my dog, a valuable brute, froze to death.

The following day proving fine and clear, we were able to continue, and on the 25th we reached Prince of Wales Fort, having been absent from it for eight months and twenty-two days upon a fruitless or at least an unsuccessful journey. Nevertheless, I was not disheartened, for with Matonabbee's assistance I was determined to start out again with the least possible delay.

On the 28th, Matonabbee and his party arrived, and I promptly offered my services to the Governor for a new excursion. The offer was readily accepted, as my abilities and approved courage in persevering under difficulties were thought adequate to the task. I immediately engaged Matonabbee as my guide, but the Governor once again attempted to force some of the Home Guard Indians upon me, for these people were his relatives and he wished that they might engross all the credit of taking care of me. However, I had found them of so little use on previous occasions that I absolutely refused them, and thereby offended Mr. Norton to such a degree that neither time nor absence could ever afterwards eradicate his dislike of me.

This Mr. Moses Norton was the son of Mr. Richard Norton, a former Governor, and of a Southern Indian woman. He was born at Prince of Wales Fort, though he subsequently spent nine years in school in England. At his return to Hudson's Bay he entered into all the abominable vices of his countrymen. He kept, for his own use, five or six of the finest Indian girls which he could select, but notwithstanding his own uncommon propensity to the fair sex, he took every means in his power to prevent the other Europeans from having intercourse with the women of the country; for which purpose he proceeded to the most ridiculous lengths. To his own friends and countrymen he was so partial that he set more value on, and showed more respect to, one of their favourite dogs than he ever did to his first officer.

Amongst his miserable and ignorant countrymen he passed for a proficient in physic, and he always kept a box of poison to administer to those who refused him their daughters or their wives.

Despite all these bad qualities, no man took more pains to inculcate virtue, morality and continence in others; always painting in the most odious colours the jealousy and revengeful disposition of the Indians should any attempt be made to violate the chastity of their women.

Lectures of this kind from a man of established virtue might have had some effect; but when they were heard from one who was known to live in open defiance of every law, human and divine, they were received with indignation, and considered as the hypocritical cant of a selfish debauchee who simply wished to engross every woman in the country to himself.

His apartments were elegant, but always crowded with his favourite Indians. At night he kept them with him, but locked the door and put the keys under his pillow so that, in the morning, and for want of necessary conveniences, his rooms were worse than a pig sty.

As he advanced in years his jealousy increased, and he actually poisoned two of his women because he thought them partial to other men more suitable to their ages. He was also a notorious smuggler, but strangely, though he put many thousands into the pockets of his Indian Captains, he seldom put a shilling in his own.

An inflammation of the bowels occasioned his death, some time after the completion of my Coppermine adventures; and though he died in the most excruciating pain, he retained his jealousy to the last. A few minutes before he expired, happening to see an officer laying hold of the hand of one of his women who was standing by, he bellowed in as loud a voice as his situation would admit:

"God damn you for a bitch! If I live, I'll knock your brains out!"

A few minutes after this elegant apostrophe he expired in the greatest agonies that can possibly be conceived.

Such was the character of Mr. Moses Norton, but to deal justly with him I must admit that on the occasion of my preparing to embark on my third journey, he fitted me out with every object that I, or Matonabbee, considered might be wanted. He then provided me with the best substitute for my broken quadrant which was then available, although it was very inferior, being an old Elton's quadrant which had been about the Fort for many years. Having given me my orders in writing, his business with me was concluded and, on the 7th of December in the year 1770, I set out on my third journey.

Considering the time of the year, the weather was for some days pretty mild; but the illness of one of Matonabbee's wives occasioned us to walk so slow that it was the 13th before we reached Seal River.

Finding deer and other game to be very scarce we now placed Matonabbee's sick wife on a sledge, and the Indians walked as far each day as their loads would permit.

On the 16th we arrived at Egg River, where Matonabbee and the rest of his crew had laid up some provisions. On reaching this place we found, to our great mortification, that some of the Indians whom the Governor had first traded with and then dispatched from the Fort, had robbed the cache of every article. The loss was severely felt, for there was a total want of game and, not expecting such a great disappointment, my Indians had not used economy in the expenditure of oatmeal and other provisions which they had received from the Fort.

Nevertheless, this loss was borne with the greatest fortitude, and I did not hear one of them breathe the least hint of revenge in case they ever found the offenders. The only effect was to make them put their best foot forward, and for some time we walked every day from morning to night. However, the days being short, the sledges heavy, and the road very bad, we seldom exceeded sixteen or eighteen miles a day.

On the 18th we saw the tracks of many deer, but none were fresh. However, some Indians who had passed this way had killed more than they required so that several joints of meat were found at their old tent-places. These, though only sufficient for one meal, were very acceptable, for we had been in exceedingly straitened circumstances for many days.

From the 19th we traversed nothing but barren ground, with our bellies empty, until the 27th when we arrived at some small woods, and some deer were killed. The Indians never ceased eating that whole day, and indeed we had been in great want, having had no morsel of food for three days past.

I must admit that I have never spent so dull a Christmas. My Indians, however, kept in good spirits, and as we began to see the fresh tracks of many deer they thought that the worst of the road was over for that winter.

We now travelled north-westward along the edge of the forests, where the trees were reduced to ill-shaped, stunted pines mingled with small dwarf junipers, until, on the 30th of December, we arrived at the frozen shore of Island Lake. The Indians killed two deer here, but the rutting season was so lately over that their flesh was hardly edible. Matonabbee was taken very ill at this place and, from the nature of his complaint, I judged his illness as resulting from the enormous quantities of meat he had eaten. It is common for these Indians, after eating as much as six men, to find themselves somewhat out of order, but none of them can ever bear to hear that their illness is the effect of over-eating.

Notwithstanding that they are voracious on occasion, yet they bear hunger with a degree of fortitude which, as has been said, "is much easier to admire than to imitate." I have often seen them, at the end of a three-day fast, as merry and jocose on the subject as if their abstinence from food had been self-imposed. They would, for instance, ask each other in the plainest terms and in the merriest mood, if they had any inclination for an intrigue with a woman.

Walking for two days to the westward on this lake we came, on the first day of 1771, to the camp which contained the families of my guides. There were upward of twenty women and children there, with only two men, and these had neither guns nor ammunition, so the whole had been subsisting on fish, and a few rabbits which they snared. Taking these people with us we marched seven miles farther, until, having passed the west shore of the lake and killed two deer, we put up for the night.

At the part where we crossed it, Island Lake is about thirty-five miles wide, but from the north-east to the south-west it is much larger. It is entirely full of islands, so near each other as to make the whole lake resemble a jumble of serpentine rivers and creeks. At different parts of this lake most of the wives and families of the Indians who visit Prince of Wales Fort in the autumn generally reside until their men return.

After leaving Island Lake we continued our course between the west and north at the easy pace of eight or nine miles a day. Provisions were scarce until January 16th, when twelve deer were killed, and we thereupon decided to remain a few days to dry some of the meat. On the 22nd we met the first stranger we had seen since leaving the Fort, though we had travelled several hundred miles, which shows how thinly this part of the country is inhabited.

It is a truth well known to the natives that there are many very extensive tracts of ground in these parts which are incapable of affording support to members of the human race even when these are in the capacity of migrants. Few of the lakes and rivers are completely destitute of fish, but the uncertainty of meeting with a sufficient supply makes the natives very cautious how they put their whole dependence on this article, as such dependence has too frequently been the means of many hundreds being starved to death.

On the 3rd of February we were again in sight of the barren ground, but as the deer still remained within the woods we altered our course to the west to remain with them.

Having got across the Cathawhachaga River we came to Cossed Whoie, or Partridge Lake, and began to cross it on the 7th. It is impossible to describe the intenseness of the cold we experienced that day, but the dispatch we made in crossing fourteen miles was almost incredible, for the greatest part of the men performed it in two hours; though the women, being heavier laden, took much longer.

Several of the Indians were frozen, but none of them more disagreeably than one of Matonabbee's wives, whose thighs and buttocks were encrusted with ice so that, when they thawed, several blisters arose which were as large as sheep's bladders. The pain the poor woman suffered was greatly aggravated by the laughter and jeering of her companions, who said that she was rightly served for belting her clothes so high. I must admit that I was not of the number who pitied her, as I thought she took too much pains to show a clean heel and a good leg; her garters always being in sight which, though not considered indecent here, is by far too airy for the rigorous cold of the severe winter in a high northern latitude.

We continued our course for many days to the west, remaining within the forests. The deer were so plentiful and the Indians killed such vast numbers that we frequently had to halt for four or five days to eat up the spoils. We often left great quantities of meat behind us, but this conduct is excusable among a wandering people, for the great uncertainty of their ever visiting these parts again makes them think there is nothing improvident in living on the best.

Since the deer continued plentiful, Matonabbee assured me that the best way we could employ ourselves until spring, when the deer would go to the barren ground and the season would permit us to follow, was to kill and eat as many deer as possible. So we continued but slowly until we came to Whold-yah'd, or Pike Lake, which is drained by the Dubawnt River. Here we met some Northern Indians who had been living there since the beginning of winter and had found a plentiful subsistence in catching deer in a pound.

When the Indians wish to build such a pound they first find a main deer path, preferably where it crosses a lake or other opening. The pound is then constructed by enclosing a circular space with a strong fence made of brushy trees. I have seen some that were a mile round, and am informed that others are even bigger. The door is no larger than a common gate, and the inside of the pound is so crowded with small counter-hedges as to resemble a maze. In every opening of these is set a snare made with thongs of deer-skin, and each snare is usually made fast to a living tree or, if these are not plentiful, to a log of such a size that the deer cannot drag it far.

The pound having been prepared, a row of small brushwood is stuck up in the snow on each side of the door and continued out on the open space, where neither stick nor stump besides is to be seen; which makes the brushwood yet more distinctly observed. These pieces of brushwood are placed at fifteen or twenty yards apart, and in such a manner as to form two sides of a long acute angle growing gradually wider as the distance from the pound increases. Sometimes the arms of the angle extend as far as two or three miles.

The Indians pitch their tents near an eminence so that they can observe the approach of the deer which, when they are seen, are driven toward the pound by the women and children. The poor, timorous deer, finding themselves thus pursued, and taking the two rows of brushwood to be rows of men, run straight down the path into the pound. The Indians then close in and block the door with brushy trees that have been cut for the purpose. Then, while the women and children walk around the pound to prevent any of the deer escaping, the men spear those animals which are ensnared, and shoot with bows and arrows any that remain loose.

This method of hunting is so successful that many families of Northern Indians subsist by it all the winter. When the spring advances, both the deer and the Indians draw out into the barren ground, and remain on the move until the following winter.

Such an easy way of procuring a comfortable mainte-nance is wonderfully well adapted to the support of the

aged and infirm, but is too apt to occasion an habitual indolence in the young, for those who indulge in this indolent method of procuring food can have small interest
in procuring furs for trade. On the other hand, those Indians who do not get their livelihood so easily, generally
procure sufficient furs to purchase ammunition and
other European goods. These last Indians are of the most
importance and value to the Hudson's Bay Company, as
it is from them the furs are procured which compose the
greatest part of the Churchill trade.

In my opinion, there cannot exist stronger proof that
mankind was not created to enjoy happiness than the
conduct of the miserable wretches who inhabit this part
of the world, for few of the Northern Indians, except the
aged and infirm, or those who are indolent or unam-
bitious, will any longer submit to remaining in the parts
where food and clothing are procured in the easy manner
of impounding deer; for the reason that they get no fur
for trade, and therefore cannot purchase what they will.

What then, do the industrious gatherers of fur gain for
their trouble? The real wants of these people are few and
easily supplied. A hatchet, ice-chisel, file and knife are all
that is required to enable them to procure a comfortable
livelihood. Those of them who endeavour to possess
more are always the most unhappy and may, in fact, be
said to be only slaves and carriers to the rest, whose am-
bition does not lead them beyond the need of procuring
food and clothing for themselves.

It is true that the more industrious Indians who carry
the furs gathered by themselves and other Indians to the
Factory, pride themselves upon the respect which we
show them at the Fort. Yet to gain this respect they frequently run great risks of being starved to death in their
way thither and back. Furthermore, all that they can
possibly get from their year's journeying and toil seldom
amounts to more than is sufficient to yield a bare subsistence; while those Indians whom we call indolent, live
in a state of plenty, without trouble and risk, and conse-

quently must be the most happy, and the most independent also. Indeed those who take no concern about gathering furs, generally have an opportunity of providing themselves with the trade goods they require by exchanging for provisions and ready-dressed skins with their more industrious countrymen.

It is undoubtedly the duty of every one of the Company's servants to encourage a spirit of industry among the natives, and to use every means in their power to induce them to procure furs; and I can truly say that this has ever been the grand object of my attention. But at the same time I must confess that such conduct is by no means for the real benefit of the poor Indians, it being well known that those who have the least intercourse with the Factories are by far the happiest.

Six

W E STOPPED only one night with these Indians and on the 4th of March began crossing the remainder of Pike Lake, a distance of only twenty-seven miles. Yet the Indians lost so much time in play that we did not reach the other side until the 7th.

On the 9th, we met with as great plenty of deer as we had seen, which no doubt made things go so smoothly as they did. On the 19th, we saw the tracks of several strangers and that night arrived at five tents of Northern Indians who had resided there the great part of the winter, snaring deer in pounds. It would seem that this place had been much frequented in the past, for the quantity of trees that had been cut for fuel and other uses was well nigh incredible.

Because of stormy weather we remained here for some days. According to my estimate we were then about five hundred miles to the westward of Prince of Wales Fort, though the distance we had travelled must have been much greater. I also embraced the opportunity of sending a letter to the Fort by the hands of some Indians who were going there in the summer.

We pursued our way on the 23rd, and during the following days saw many Northern Indians employed with pounds. Some of them joined our crew and proceeded with us to the westward until, on April 8th, we arrived at a small lake called Theleweyaza Yeth, or Lake of the Little Fish Hill. Finding deer very numerous hereabouts, the Indians determined to halt to dry and pound meat, for it would soon be the season for the deer to withdraw northward to the barren ground and it was uncertain when we would meet them again.

Our numbers had now increased to not less than seventy people who, during our ten-day stay at Theleweyaza Yeth, were employed in preparing meat, and in making small staves of birch-wood about one and a quarter inches square and seven or eight feet long. These were to serve as tent poles all the summer on the barren ground, and would then be converted into snowshoe frames. Birch bark, together with wood for building canoes, was also gathered at this place, for beyond Theleweyaza Yeth there are few good stands of birch to be had. All of this woodwork was reduced to proper size for easy carriage, for it was not proposed to build the canoes until we had gone north to Lake Clowey on the edge of the barren ground.

On the 18th of April we set out northward, but had gone only ten miles when we came to the tent of some Northern Indians from whom Matonabbee purchased another wife; so that he now had no less than seven, most of whom, for size, would have made good grenadiers.

He prided himself much on the height and strength of his wives, and would frequently say that few women could carry or haul heavier loads. Though they had a most masculine appearance, he preferred them to those of a more delicate form. Indeed, in a country like this, where a partner in excessive hard labour is the chief motive for the union, and where the softer endearments of a conjugal life are only considered as a secondary object, there seemed to be great propriety in such a choice.

But if all the men were of this way of thinking, what would become of the greater part of the women, who in general are but of low stature, and many of them of the most delicate make? However, taken in a body, the women of these Indians are as destitute of real beauty as any nation I ever saw, although there are some few of them who, when young, are tolerable enough. But the care of a family makes the most beautiful of them look old and wrinkled before they are thirty, and the appearances of several of the more ordinary ones of that age are perfect antidotes to love and gallantry. This, however, does not render them less dear to their owners, which is a lucky thing for these women, and a certain proof that there is no such thing as any general standard of beauty in the world.

Ask a Northern Indian what is beauty, and he will answer: a broad, flat face, small eyes, high cheek-bones, three or four black lines across each cheek, a tawny hide – and breasts hanging down to the belt.

These beauteous attributes are rendered more valuable when the possessor is also capable of dressing all kinds of skins, of converting them into clothing, and of carrying a hundred-and-forty-pound load on her back in summer, or hauling a much greater one in winter.

The temper of the women is of little consequence, for the men have an admirable facility in making the most stubborn comply with great alacrity to their wishes.

In general the women are kept at a great distance and have a very low rank. Even the wives and daughters of the Captains are never served their food until all the men, including those who are in the capacity of servants, have eaten their fill. Consequently, in times of famine, it is frequently these women's lot to be left without a morsel. It is natural, however, to think that they take the liberty of helping themselves in secret; but this must be done with great prudence, as discovery subjects them to severe beatings.

Their marriages are not attended with any ceremony, and matches are usually made by the parents or next of kin. The women seem to implicitly obey the will of their parents, who endeavour to marry their daughters to those who seem most likely to be able to support the parents in old age, even though the years, person, or disposition of these prospective husbands be ever so despicable.

The girls are betrothed as children, but never to those

of equal age, which is doubtless sound policy in a place where the existence of a family depends entirely on the abilities and industry of a single man. Thus it is very common to see men of thirty-five or forty years with wives of ten or twelve, and sometimes younger.

From the age of eight or nine years, the girls are prohibited from joining in the most innocent amusements with male children. When sitting in their tents, or even when travelling, they are watched and guarded with an unremitting vigilance that cannot be exceeded by the most rigid discipline of an English boarding-school. Fortunately, custom makes such restraints sit lightly on them.

Notwithstanding these uncommon restraints on the young girls, the conduct of their parents is by no means consistent with this plan. They set no bounds to their conversation, but talk before the children, and even to them, on the most indelicate subjects. However, as the young are accustomed to this, it does not have the same effect upon them as it would in a civilized country where every care is taken to prevent their morals from being contaminated by obscene conversation.

Divorces are pretty common; sometimes for incontinency, but more frequently for want of what they deem the necessary accomplishments, or for bad behaviour. The ceremony of divorce consists of nothing more nor less than a good drubbing and then turning the woman out of doors, telling her to go to her paramour or her relations, according to the nature of the crime.

Providence is kind in causing these people to be less prolific than the inhabitants of civilized nations. It is uncommon for a woman to have more than five or six children, and these are usually born at such a distance from one another that the youngest may be two or three years old before the next arrives. They make no use of cradles, but tie a lump of moss between the baby's legs, and carry the children on their backs, next to their skin, until they are able to walk.

There are certain periods when the women are not permitted to abide in the same tent with the men. At such times they must make a small hovel for themselves some distance from the tents. This universal custom is also a favoured policy with the women who, after a difference with their husbands, make it an excuse for a temporary separation. The use of this custom is so prevalent that I have known some sulky dames to leave their husbands and their tents for four or five days at a time, and repeat the farce twice or thrice a month, while the poor men have never suspected the deceit – or, if they have, delicacy has not permitted them to inquire into the matter. I once knew Matonabbee's handsome wife to live apart from him for several weeks, under this pretence. He, however, had some suspicions, for she was carefully watched to prevent her giving her company to another man.

Women in this condition are never permitted to walk on the ice of rivers or lakes, or near the part where the men are hunting beaver, or have a fishing net, for fear of averting their success. They are also prohibited at those times from eating the head of any animals and from walking in, or crossing over, the track where the head of an animal has lately been carried by a hunter.

The 21st was the day appointed for moving this camp, but one of the women having been taken in labour, and it being rather an extraordinary case, we were detained two days. However, the instant the poor woman was delivered, after having suffered the birth pangs for fifty-two hours, the signal was made for moving. The poor creature then took her infant on her back and set out with the rest of our company. Though another person had the humanity to haul her sledge for her, for one day only, she was obliged to carry a considerable load, in addition to her little charge, and was frequently required to wade knee deep in water and wet snow. Her very looks, exclusive of her moans, were sufficient proof of the great pain she endured. Though she was a person I greatly disliked, I never felt more for any of her sex in all my life; indeed her sighs pierced me to the soul and rendered me very miserable, as it was not in my power to relieve her.

When a Northern Indian woman is taken in labour at some fixed camp, a small tent is erected for her at such a distance from the others that her cries cannot easily be heard. No male, except children in arms, is ever allowed to approach her. It is a circumstance perhaps to be lamented that these people never attempt to assist one another on these occasions even in the most critical cases. This is probably owing to the opinion they entertain that nature is sufficiently able to perform what is required without external help.

When I informed them of the assistance which European women get from midwives, they treated it with the utmost contempt, ironically observing that the many hump-backs, bandy-legs, and other deformities so frequent amongst the whites, were undoubtedly owing to the great skill of the persons who assisted in bringing them into the world, and to the extraordinary care of their nurses afterwards.

After child-birth a Northern woman is reckoned unclean for a month or five weeks, during which time she remains in her little tent. During this time the father never sees the child. The reason for this is that children, when first born, are not very sightly, having in general large heads and but little hair, and moreover, being often discoloured by the force of labour; so that were the father to see them at this disadvantage, he might probably take a dislike to them which would never afterwards be removed.

On the 23rd of April, as I have said, we had begun to move north. The weather had now begun to grow so hot, and so much snow melted, that it made bad walking in snowshoes, and such exceedingly heavy hauling that it was the 3rd of May before we reached the Lake Clowey.

This lake is only about twelve miles broad in its widest part and is said to drain westward into Lake Athapuscow. It is a famous collecting-place for Indians proceeding to the barren ground, for it is the last place with good woods about it, and it is here that they halt to build their canoes. The same day that we arrived, several other Indians joined us from various quarters and, before we left, upwards of two hundred Indians had come.

Their canoes are very singular, being so small and light, and so simple in their construction, as to somewhat resemble the kayaks used by the Eskimos. Their chief use is to ferry over rivers, although they are sometimes used in the spearing of deer as these swim across a narrow place, and they are also useful for killing swans and geese in the moulting season. This kind of canoe is only built to use upon the barren grounds in summer, and not for river travel.

All the tools used by the Indians in building their sledges and canoes, as well as in making snowshoes and all other kinds of woodwork, consist of a hatchet, a knife, a file and an awl. Yet they are so dexterous that everything they make is executed with a neatness not to be excelled by the most expert mechanic assisted with every tool he could wish.

The tents made use of by the Northern Indians, for both summer and winter, are generally composed of deer-skin with hair attached and, for convenience of carriage, are always made in small pieces. These tents, as also their pots and some other light lumber, are carried by pack dogs which are trained to that service. The dogs are of various sizes and colours, but are all of the fox and wolf breeds, with sharp noses, full, bushy tails and sharp upstanding ears. They are of great courage and bite so sharp that the smallest cur amongst them will keep several of our large English dogs at bay, if he can get in a corner. The dogs are equally willing to haul on the sledges, but as few of the Indians will take the trouble of making dog sledges, the poor women must remain content with carrying the heavy weights, while lessening the bulk of their loads by lashing the lighter articles to the dogs' backs.

In the fall of the year, with the advance of winter, the people sew the skins of deer's legs together in the shape of a long portmanteau, which is as slippery as an otter when hauled over the snow, and which serves as a temporary sledge while in the barren grounds.

Once within the woods again, they make proper sledges, using boards from the larch tree. These boards are about a quarter of an inch thick, and seldom exceed five or six inches in width. If they were broader they would be very unhandy to work. They are sewn together with thongs of deer-skin, and several cross-bars of wood are sewn on the upper side, both to strengthen the sled and to secure the ground lashings to which the load is fastened. The head of the sledge is turned up to form a semicircle, which prevents the carriage from diving into light snow, and enables it to rise over inequalities. The trace is a double string, and the bight is put across the shoulder of the person hauling, so as to rest against the breast.

The snowshoes these people make differ from all others, for they are so shaped that the inner sides of the frames are almost straight, while the outer sides have a wide sweep. Therefore each one of a pair is not interchangeable from left to right foot or vice versa.

There were now very many Indians at Clowey, but since I was under the protection of a principal man I was not molested, nor were they clamorous for anything I had. This was well, for notwithstanding that we had advanced so small a portion of our journey, yet more than half my store of tobacco was already expended.

Gunpowder and shot were articles commonly in demand and, in general, these were dealt round with a liberal hand by Matonabbee. I must, however, do him the justice to add that what he distributed was his own property which he had purchased at the Factory. To my certain knowledge .he bartered 150 marten skins for powder alone, besides a great number of beaver and other furs for shot, iron work and tobacco, purposely to give away among his countrymen.

On the 20th of May we had left Clowey and were proceeding northward when a gang of strangers joined us with the information that Captain Keelshies was within a day's walk to the southward. I had not seen nor heard of Keelshies since I had sent a letter for supplies by him to the Fort the previous year, so Matonabbee dispatched two young men to bring him after us, with the goods which he might have for us.

In three days we had passed beyond the range of living trees, though we still saw patches of dead and blasted wood. I have observed, during several journeys, that all the way from the Seal River the edge of the forest is faced with old, withered stumps and blasted trees that sometimes extend twenty miles from the living woods; which is proof that the cold has been increasing in these parts for some ages.

Our travels were now far from pleasant, for the weather one day was fine and hot, and the next day we had snow and thick drifting sleet, or intense cold and frost; and since we were now beyond the trees, there was but little shelter.

On the 28th we were on the ice of the large lake called Peshew, and here the Indians proposed to rest until Captain Keelshies caught up to us. During the night one of Matonabbee's wives, and another woman, eloped. It was supposed that they went off eastward in order to meet their former husbands, from whom they had been taken by force.

The affair made more noise and bustle than I could have supposed, and Matonabbee seemed entirely disconcerted and was quite inconsolable. In truth the wife he had lost seemed to have every good quality that could render her an agreeable companion in this part of the world. She had, however, chosen to return to a sprightly young fellow of no note who had been her former husband, rather than to have the seventh share of the affection of the greatest man in the country.

I am sorry to mention it, but at Clowey Lake Matonabbee did a great crime to this woman's husband, and for no other reason than that the poor man had spoken disrespectfully about Matonabbee for taking his wife from him. Matonabbee had no sooner heard of the man's arrival near our camp at Clowey Lake than he took out his knife, went into the man's tent, and without any preface, took him by the collar and began to execute his horrid design. The poor man, anticipating his danger, fell on his face and called for help, but before it came he had received three wounds in his back which, fortunately for him, all happened on the shoulder blade.

Matonabbee returned to his tent afterwards, sat down composedly, lit his pipe, and asked me if I did not think he had done right. In matters concerning his women, he was by no means free of the worst human passions.

It has always been the custom of these people to wrestle for any woman to whom they are attached and, of course, the strongest man generally carries off the prize. A weak man, unless he be a good hunter and well beloved, is seldom permitted to keep a wife that a stronger man thinks is worth his notice; for at any time when the present wives of these strong men are overladen, such men make no scruple of tearing another man's wife from his bosom, to make her bear a part of their luggage.

This custom causes a great spirit of emulation among the youth who are, upon all occasions from their childhood, constantly trying their strength and skill at wrestling. Such training helps protect their wives from the hands of those powerful ravishers, some of whom make a livelihood by taking what they want from the weaker parties, without making any return.

The way in which they tear the woman and other property from one another, though it has the appearance of great brutality, can hardly be called fighting. I never

knew any of them to receive the least hurt in these en-
counters, for the whole business seems to consist of hauling each other about by the hair of the head; and they are
seldom known either to strike or kick one another.

It is not uncommon for one of them to cut off his hair
and grease his ears immediately before the contest begins,
and this he does secretly in his own tent. It is then very
laughable to see the challenger strutting about outside
with an air of great importance, shouting "Where is he?
Why does he not come out and wrestle with me?" Where-
upon the other will bolt out with clean-shorn head and
greased ears, rush on his antagonist, seize him by the hair
and, though often a weaker man, drag him to the ground,
while the other poor fellow cannot get a grip at all.

No one ever interferes with these trials of strength and
cunning which, in the main, are very fair. Nevertheless it
was often very unpleasant for me to see the object of such
a contest sitting in pensive silence waiting her fate, while
her husband and his rival contended for her. I have indeed felt the utmost indignation when I have seen them
won, perhaps by a man they mortally hated. On these occasions their reluctance to follow their new lord has often
ended in the greatest brutality, and I have seen the poor
girls stripped naked and carried by main force to their
new lodging.

At other times it was pleasant enough to see a fine girl
led off from a husband she disliked, with a tear in one
eye, and her finger on the other.

Seven

EARLY ON the morning of the 29th of May, Captain Keelshies joined us. He delivered a two-quart keg of French brandy and a packet of letters to me, which he had carried with him for many months; but the powder, shot, tobacco and knives which he had got at the Fort for me were all expended. He apologized for this by explaining that some of his relations had died in the winter and, according to custom, he had thrown away all his own things as a form of mourning, after which he was obliged to have recourse to my goods to support his numerous family. As a small recompense for my loss he presented me with four ready-dressed moose skins, which were in reality very acceptable to me on account of their great use as moccasin leather, which at that time was a very scarce article with us.

On this same day an Indian man, who had been some time in our company, insisted on taking one of Matonabbee's wives by force, unless Matonabbee should give him a certain quantity of ammunition, some ironwork, a kettle, and other objects. All these Matonabbee was obliged to deliver or lose the woman, for he could not hope to out-wrestle the other man, who far excelled him in strength. Matonabbee was the more exasperated as the man had sold him this same woman no longer ago than the preceding month.

This dispute was likely to prove fatal to my expedition,

for Matonabbee, who had thought himself as great a man as ever lived, took this affront so much to heart (especially as it was offered in my presence) that he was on the point of striking off to the westward to join the Athapuscow Indians who, he said, would treat him with more civility than his countrymen ever did.

I now had every apprehension that my third journey would end as the others had, but after waiting till his passion had abated, I used every argument in favour of his proceeding on the journey. In particular I assured him that the Hudson's Bay Company would be most ready to acknowledge his assiduity in conducting a business which had so much appearance of proving advantageous to them.

After a good deal of entreaty he at last consented to proceed. Though it was then late afternoon, he gave orders for moving, and accordingly we walked seven miles before putting up at an island in Peshew Lake. That day we saw our first deer since leaving the vicinity of Theleweyaza Yeth; we had been subsisting meanwhile on dried meat.

On the last day of May we reached the north end of Peshew Lake, and now Matonabbee made all the arrangements to speed our design to reach the copper mines. He selected two of his young wives, who had no children, to accompany us forward, while the rest of the women and children of the party were to proceed northward at their leisure and, at a particular place in the barren grounds, await our return from the Coppermine River. We then made all our loads as light as possible, taking no more ammunition than was needed for our support, and by the next evening were ready to proceed toward our goal.

The women we had left behind set up a most piteous yelling as long as we were within earshot, but this mournful scene had so little effect on my party that they walked away laughing, and as merry as ever.

Though it was late at night when we started, we walked

ten miles before halting, and the Indians killed several deer. To talk of travelling and killing deer in the middle of the night may have the appearance of romance, but we were then so far north that, even at midnight, the sun was hardly below the horizon.

I must now return to another event which occurred at Lake Clowey, for during our stay at that place a great number of Indians had entered into combination with my party to accompany us to the Coppermine River, with no other intent than to murder the Eskimos who are understood to frequent that river in numbers. This scheme, notwithstanding the danger and hardship which attended it, was so universally approved that almost every man who joined us proposed to be one of the war party.

Accordingly, each volunteer prepared a target, or shield, before we left Clowey. These were composed of thin boards, two feet broad and three feet long, and were intended to ward off the arrows of the Eskimos.

However, when the time came to go, only sixty volunteers remained firm in their resolve. The rest, reflecting that they had a great distance to walk and that no advantage could be gained from the expedition, prudently begged to be excused. But had they possessed as many European goods as Matonabbee did, in all probability many of these men might have been glad to accompany us.

When I first heard of these plans I endeavoured to persuade the Indians against putting their inhuman design into execution; but it was concluded by them that I was only actuated by cowardice, and they told me, with great derision, that I was afraid of the Eskimos. As I knew that my personal safety depended on the favourable opinion they entertained of me, I was obliged to change my tone. I replied that I did not care if they rendered the Eskimos extinct and, though I did not see the necessity of attacking them without cause, yet so far from being afraid of a poor Eskimo, whom I despised more than feared, nothing should be wanting on my part to protect all those who were with me.

This declaration was received with great satisfaction, and I never afterwards ventured to interfere with their war plans, for to have done so would have been the height of folly for a man in my position.

Nor was the blood thirst of the Indians entirely without justification, even though this was laid in superstition. It is their belief that, when any of the principal Northern Indians dies, it is because he has been conjured to death by one of their own countrymen, by some of the Southern Indians, or by the Eskimos. Too frequently the suspicion falls on the latter tribe, which is the chief reason for the Indians never being at peace with those poor people.

For some time past, those Eskimos who trade with our sloops at Knapp's Bay, Navel's Bay, and Whale Cove north of the Churchill River, have been in peace and friendship with the Northern Indians; which is owing to the protection they have received for several years past from the Chiefs at Prince of Wales Fort. But in the summer of 1756, a party of Northern Indians lay in wait at Knapp's Bay till the sloop had sailed out of the harbour, when they fell upon the Eskimos and killed every soul. Mr. John Bean, Master of the sloop, heard the guns very plain, but did not know the meaning of it until the following summer when he found the shocking remains of more than forty Eskimos who had been murdered at Knapp's Bay, for no other reason than because two principal Northern Indians had died in the preceding winter.

In places far to the north, that do not have any intercourse with our vessels, the Eskimos very often continue to fall a sacrifice to the fury and superstition of the Northern Indians; though these are by no means a bold and warlike people. Nor can I think, from experience, that they are particularly guilty of committing such acts of wanton cruelty on any other part of the human race except the Eskimos.

Without the encumbrance of the women and children, we travelled northward at great speed, but the weather was so precarious, and the snow, sleet and rain so frequent, that it was the 16th of June before we arrived at Cogead Lake, where the women and children were to meet us on our return.

On our way to this place we crossed several large lakes on the ice, including Thoynoykyed and Thoycoylyned, together with a few rivers and creeks. The deer were plentiful, and the Indians killed great numbers, frequently only for the fat, marrow, and tongues. I tried to convince them of the great impropriety of such waste but, as national customs are not easily overcome, my remonstrances proved ineffectual. They replied that it was right to kill plenty and live on the best, for it would be impossible to do this when the game was scarce.

From the 17th to the 20th of June, we walked eighty miles to the north, mostly on the ice of Cogead Lake.

On the 22nd we arrived at the banks of Congecathawhachaga River where we met some Copper Indians who were assembled, according to their annual custom, to kill the deer which cross the river there.

The ice now being broken, we were obliged to make use of our canoes for the first time, to ferry across this river; which would have proved very tedious had it not been for the kindness of the Copper Indians who sent their own canoes to our assistance. For, though our number was nearly 150, we had only three canoes, and these could only carry two persons each, without baggage. In some cases the Northern Indians lash three or four canoes together to make a raft which will carry a much greater weight, but this can only be done when the water is quite smooth.

Having arrived on the north side, we discovered that Matonabbee and several others of our company were acquainted with most of the Copper Indians whom we found there. The latter seemed highly pleased by our presence and assured us of their readiness to serve to the utmost. By the time we had our tents pitched, the strangers had provided a large quantity of dry meat and fat, by way of a feast.

No sooner had the Copper Indians been made acquainted with the warlike nature of our journey than they expressed complete approbation. They even offered to lend us several canoes which, they assured us, would prove useful in the remaining part of our journey.

I smoked my *calumet*, or peace pipe, with their principal men, and I must confess that their civility far exceeded what I had thought to expect from so uncivilized a tribe. I was sorry that I had nothing of value to offer them, for, though they have some European commodities which they purchase from the Northern Indians, the same articles from the hand of an Englishman were more highly prized.

As I was the first white man they had ever seen, and would in all probability be the last, it was curious how they flocked around me, expressing as much desire to examine me from top to toe as a European naturalist would a non-descript animal.

They found and pronounced me to be a perfect human being, except in the colour of my hair and eyes. The former, they said, was like the stained hair of a buffalo's tail; the latter, being light, were like those of a gull. The whiteness of my skin was, in their opinion, no ornament, as they said it resembled meat which had been sodden in water till all the blood was extracted.

As Matonabbee and the others thought it advisable to leave at this place the few women we had brought with us, it was necessary for us to remain here a few days to kill as many deer as would be needed for their support.

We had not been many days at Congecathawhachaga before I had reason to be greatly concerned at the behaviour of certain of my crew toward the Copper Indians. They not only took many of their young women, furs, and ready-dressed skins, but also several of their bows and arrows, which were the only implements they had to procure food and raiment.

To do Matonabbee justice, he endeavoured to make his countrymen give a satisfactory return for the material things they took; but he did not hinder them from taking as many women as they pleased. Indeed the Copper Indian women seem to be much esteemed by our Northern Indians, for what reason I know not, as they are in reality the same people in every respect.

In my opinion no race of people under the sun have a greater occasion for indulging in a plurality of wives than the Northern Indians. Their annual haunts, in quest of fur, are so remote from any European settlement as to render them the greatest travellers in the known world. As they have no horses, or water carriage, every good hunter is under the necessity of having several persons to assist in carrying his furs to the Company's fort, as well as carrying back European goods. No persons in this country are so proper for this work as the women, because they are inured to carry and haul heavy loads from childhood, and to do all manner of drudgery. Thus it is that men who are capable of providing for five, six, or more women, generally find them humble and faithful servants, affectionate wives, and fond and indulgent mothers to their children.

Much does it redound to the honour of the Northern Indian women when I affirm that they are the mildest and most virtuous females I have seen in any part of North America. However, when any of them have been permitted to remain at the Fort they have, for the sake of gain, been easily prevailed on to deviate from that character; and a few have come to be as abandoned as the Southern Indians, who are remarkable for being the most debauched wretches under the sun. So far from laying any restraint on their sensual appetites they do, as long as youth and inclination last, give themselves up to all manner of even incestuous debauchery, and that in so beastly a manner, when intoxicated, that the brute creation are not less regardful of decency.

The Northern Indian women are so far from being like their Southern sisters that it is very uncommon to hear of their being guilty of incontinency, even when they are confined to the sixth or seventh part of a husband.

It may appear strange that, while I am extolling the chastity of the Northern Indian women, I should acknowledge that it is a very common custom amongst the men of this country to exchange a night's lodging with each other's wives. This is so far from being considered a criminal act that it is esteemed by them as one of the strongest ties of friendship between two families, and in the case of the death of either man, the other considers himself bound to support the children of the deceased.

They are so far from viewing this obligation as a mere ceremony (as do most of our Christian god-parents who, notwithstanding their vows, scarcely ever afterwards remember what they have promised) that there is not an instance known to me of a Northern Indian neglecting the duties which he has accepted towards the children of his friend.

Though the Northern Indians make no scruple of having two or three sisters for wives at the same time, they are most particular about observing the proper distance in the consanguinity of those who have intercourse with their wives. The Southern Indians are far less scrupulous, and it is common for one brother to make free with another's wife or daughter. It is also notorious that many of them cohabit occasionally with their own mothers, and frequently espouse sisters and daughters.

Eight

O N   T H E   S E C O N D of July the weather began very ill, with much snow and sleet; but about nine o'clock at night it grew more moderate and so we set out and walked about ten miles to the north by west, when we lay down to take a little sleep. Several of our Indians had chosen to withdraw from the war lists and stay at Congecathawha-chaga with the women, but their loss was amply supplied by Copper Indians who accompanied us in the double capacity of guides and warriors.

On the 3rd, the weather was again very bad, but we made shift to walk ten or eleven miles until we were obliged to put up because of not being able to see, due to the drifting snow. By putting up, no more is to be understood than that we got to leeward of a great stone, or into the crevices of the rocks, where we smoked our pipes or went to sleep until the weather permitted us to proceed.

Although there was a constant light snow on the 4th, which made it very disagreeable underfoot, we nevertheless managed to walk twenty-seven miles to the north-west, fourteen of which were over the Stony Mountains.

Surely no part of the world better deserves this name. When we first approached these mountains they appeared to be a vast and confused heap of rocks, utterly inaccessible to the foot of man. But having some Copper Indians with us, who knew the road, we made a tolerable shift to get on, though not without being frequently obliged to crawl on our hands and knees. Despite the intricacy of the road, there is a visible path the whole way across these mountains, even in the most difficult parts. In places it is as clear as an English foot-path, by reason of the great stretch of ages during which parties of Indians have gone over the mountains to reach the copper mines. By the side of the path there are several flat tablestones which are covered with thousands of small pebbles. The Copper Indians say these have resulted from a universal custom which requires everyone who passes this way to add a pebble to the heap. Each of us added a small stone in order to increase the number, for luck.

At the foot of the Stony Mountains, three of our Indians turned back after observing that, from every appearance, the remainder of the journey seemed likely to be attended by more trouble than would be counterbalanced by going to war with the Eskimos.

On the 5th, the weather was so bad, with constant sleet, snow and rain, that we could not see our way and so did not attempt to move. The next day we made about eleven miles to the north-west, and again had to look for shelter among the rocks. The morning after that, fifteen more Indians deserted us, being quite sick of the road and the uncommon badness of the weather.

Indeed, though these people are inured to any hardship, yet their complaint upon this occasion was not without reason. From our leaving Congecathawhachaga we scarcely had a dry garment of any kind, nor anything to screen us from the inclemency of the weather, except rocks and caves. The best of these were but damp and unwholesome lodging, and we had not been able to make one spark of fire except what was sufficient to light a pipe.

This night we had no sooner entered our retreats amongst the rocks, to eat our supper of raw venison, than a very sudden and heavy gale of wind came upon us, attended by a great fall of snow. The flakes were so large as to surpass all credibility, and they fell in such vast quantities for nine hours that we were in danger of being smothered in our caves.

On the 7th, a fresh breeze and some showers of rain, with some warm sunshine, dissolved the greatest part of the snow and we crawled out of our holes and walked about twenty miles to the north-west by west. On our way we crossed on the ice over part of a large lake, which was still far from being thawed. This lake I distinguished as Buffalo or Musk-Ox Lake, from the number of these animals that we found grazing on its margin. The Indians killed many of them but, finding them lean, took only some of the bulls' hides for moccasin soles. At night the bad weather returned, with a gale of wind and very cold rain and sleet.

This was the first time we had seen any of the musk-oxen since we had left the Factory, although I saw a great many during my first and second journeys. They are also found at times in considerable numbers near the coast of Hudson's Bay, all the way from Knapp's Bay to Wager Water; but they are most plentiful within the Arctic Circle.

In these high latitudes I have frequently seen many herds of them in the course of a day's walk, and some of those herds contained eighty or a hundred head. The number of bulls is very few in proportion to the cows, for it is rare to see more than two or three full-grown bulls with the largest herd. From the number of males that are found dead, the Indians are of the opinion that they kill each other contending for the females.

In the rutting season they are so jealous of the cows that they run at either man or beast who offers to approach them, and have even been observed to run and bellow at ravens which chanced to light near them.

They delight in the most stony and mountainous part of the barren ground. Though they are beasts of great magnitude, and apparently of very unwieldly and inactive structure, yet they climb the rocks with great ease and agility, and are nearly as sure-footed as a goat. They will feed on anything, though they seem fondest of grass. In winter they will eat moss or any other herbage they can find, as well as the tops of willows and the tender branches of the pine tree. The cows take the bull in August, and bring forth their young at the latter end of May or the beginning of June. They never have more than one calf at a time.

When full grown the musk-ox is as large as the middling size of English black cattle, but their legs are not so long; nor is their tail longer than a bear's, and it is entirely hid by the long hair of the rump and hind quarters. Their hair is, in many parts, very long; but the longest hair about them, particularly the bulls, is under the throat, extending from the chin to the lower part of the chest. It hangs down like a horse's mane inverted, and is fully as long, which gives the animal a most formidable appearance.

In winter they are provided with a thick, fine wool, which grows at the root of the long hair and shields them from the intense cold. As summer advances this wool loosens from the skin and drops off.

The flesh of the musk-ox resembles that of the western buffalo, but is more like that of the moose or elk. The calves and young heifers are good eating, but the flesh of the bulls both smells and tastes so strong of musk as to render it very disagreeable. Even the knife that cuts the flesh of an old bull will smell so strong that nothing but scouring the blade quite bright can remove it. Though no part of a bull is free from this smell, yet the parts of generation, in particular the urethra, are by far the most strongly impregnated. The urine itself must contain the scent to a very great degree, for the sheath of the penis is corroded with a brown, gummy substance which is nearly as high-scented as that produced by the civet cat and, having been kept several years, seems to lose none of its quality.

On the 8th of July the weather was more moderate, though still with rain showers, and we walked eighteen miles to the north, when the Indians killed some deer and put up by the side of a small creek which provided some willows. These were the first we had seen since leaving Congecathawhachaga, and so it was here we had our first cooked meal for a whole week. This was well relished by all parties and, as the sun had dried our clothing, we felt more comfortable than at any time since leaving the women.

The place where we lay that night is not far from Grizzled Bear Hill, which takes its name from the numbers of those animals which are known to resort thither to bear their young in a cave. The wonderful description given of this place by the Copper Indians so excited the curiosity of my companions and myself that we went to view it. On our arrival we found a high lump of earth, of loamy quality, which with several others of its kind stands in the middle of a large marsh, like so many islands in a lake. The sides of these islands are quite perpendicular and the largest is about twenty feet high. They are excellent places of refuge for birds, which nest upon their level tops in perfect safety from every beast except the wolverine or quickhatch.

We saw a cave that had evidently been occupied by the bears, but it did not interest me half so much as the sight of the many hills and dry ridges to the east which had been turned over like ploughed land by these animals in their search for ground-squirrels, which constitute a favourite part of their food. At first I thought these long and deep furrows, out of which some enormous stones had been rolled, were the work of lightning; but the Indians assured me it was entirely the work of the Grizzled Bears.

During the next two days we walked sixty miles, in weather that was sometimes cold and wet, and at others very hot and sultry; but the mosquitoes were always uncommonly numerous, and their stings almost insufferable. On the 10th, Matonabbee sent several Indians ahead with orders to proceed as fast as possible to the Coppermine River and acquaint any Indians they might meet of our approach.

On the 11th we met a Northern Indian called Oule-eye, in company with some Copper Indians, killing deer with bows-and-arrows and spears as the animals crossed a little river. I smoked my *calumet* with them but found them a different set of people from those at Congecatha-whachaga, for though they had plenty of provisions they did not offer us a mouthful. They would certainly have robbed me of the last garment from my back had I not been protected.

Bows and arrows, though the original weapons of these Northern Indians, are, since the introduction of firearms, becoming less used except in killing deer at crossing-places, or as they walk or run through a narrow pass prepared for their reception. This latter method of hunting is only practicable on the barren ground, where there is an extensive prospect enabling the hunters to see the herds at a distance, as well as to discover the nature of the country.

When the Indians prepare to hunt in this manner, they first observe the direction of the wind, and go down to leeward of the herd. They then search out a convenient place where those who are to do the shooting may hide. This done, a large bundle of sticks, like ramrods (which they carry with them the whole summer for this purpose) are ranged in two ranks to form the sides of a very acute angle; the sticks being placed at a distance of fifteen or twenty yards apart, rather in the same manner that the fences are constructed for deer pounds in the winter. The women and boys then separate into two parties and make a great circuit to get behind the deer, when they form a crescent and drive the animals toward the arms of the angle. As each of the sticks has a pennant fastened to it, which is easily moved by the wind, and a lump of moss stuck on top, the poor timorous deer probably take them for lines of people, and run straight between the two ranks. As they approach the point of the angle, the Indians in hiding rise up and begin to shoot, but as the deer generally pass at full speed they seldom have time to fire more than one or two arrows unless the herd is very large.

This method of hunting is not always attended with success, for the deer will sometimes make off another way, before the women and children can surround them. At other times, however, I have seen eleven or twelve deer killed with one volley of arrows.

The next day my companions took what provisions they wanted from the unsociable strangers, and we walked fifteen miles, in expectation of finally reaching the Coppermine River that day. But when we had reached the top of a long chain of hills through which the river was said to run, we found it to be no more than a branch which emptied into the main stream about forty miles from its influx into the sea.

At that time all our Copper Indians were dispatched on various tasks in different directions, and there was no one left who knew the shortest cut to the river; but seeing some woods to the westward, we directed our course toward them. The Indians now destroyed several fine bucks and we enjoyed the luxury of cooking them over abundant fires, for these were the first woods we had seen since shortly after leaving Clowey Lake.

As such favourable opportunities for indulging the appetite happen but seldom, we did not neglect any art, in dressing our food, which the most refined skill of Indian cookery has been able to invent. These consist chiefly of boiling, broiling and roasting, but also of a dish called *beeatee*, which is most delicious. It is made with the blood, a good quantity of fat (shredded small), some of the tenderest flesh, and the heart and the lungs torn into small shivers. All of this is put in the deer's stomach and roasted by being suspended before the fire. When it is sufficiently done it will emit steam, which is as much as to say, "Come and eat me now!"

This preparation is somewhat related to the most remarkable dish known to both the Northern and Southern Indians, which is made of blood mixed with the half-digested food found in the deer's stomach, and which is then boiled to the consistency of pease-porridge. Some fat and scraps of tender flesh are also boiled with it. To render this dish more palatable, they have a method of mixing the blood with the stomach contents in the paunch itself, and then hanging it up in the heat and smoke of the fire for several days. This puts the whole mass into a state of fermentation, and gives it such an agreeably acid taste that, were it not for prejudice, it might be eaten by those who have the nicest palates.

It is true that some people with delicate stomachs would not be persuaded to partake of this dish if they saw it being prepared, for most of the fat is first chewed by the men and boys in order to break the globules, so that it will all boil out and mingle with the broth. To do justice, however, to their cleanliness in this particular, I must observe that neither old people with bad teeth, nor young children, have any hand in preparing this dish.

At first, I must admit that I was rather shy of partaking of this mess; but when I was sufficiently convinced of the truth of the above statement, I no longer made any scruple, but always thought it exceedingly good.

The stomach of no other large animal, except the deer, is eaten by the Indians bordering Hudson's Bay. In the winter, when the deer feed on fine white moss, the contents are so much esteemed that I have often seen them sit around a fresh-killed deer and eat the contents warm out of its stomach. In summer the deer feed more coarsely, and therefore this dish, if it deserves the appellation, is not then so much in favour.

Young calves, fawns, and beaver, taken from the bellies of their mothers, are all reckoned most delicate food, and I am not the only European who heartily joins in pronouncing them the greatest dainties that can be eaten. The same may be said of young geese and ducks in the shell. In fact, it has become almost a proverb in the northern settlements that whoever wishes to know what is good, must live with the Indians.

The parts of generation belonging to any beast they kill, both male and female, are always eaten by the men and boys. Although those parts, particularly in the males, are generally very tough, they must not on any account be cut with an edge-tool, but must be torn to pieces with the teeth. When any part proves too tough to be masticated, it is thrown into the fire and burnt, for the Indians believe that if a dog should eat any of the generative parts, it would have an adverse effect upon their hunting.

They are also remarkably fond of the womb of the buffalo, elk, deer, etc., which are eagerly devoured without washing, or any other process but barely stroking out the contents. This, in some of the larger animals, and especially when they are some time gone with young, needs no description to make it sufficiently disgusting. Yet I have known some men in the Company's service who were remarkably fond of the dish; though I am not of their number. The womb of the beaver and deer is well enough, but that of moose and buffalo is very rank.

The tripe of the buffalo is exceedingly good, and the Indian method of preparing it is infinitely superior to that of the Europeans. When opportunity permits, they will wash it tolerably clean in cold water, strip off the honey-comb, and only boil it for about half or three-quarters of an hour. In that time it is sufficiently done for eating and, though rather tougher than what is prepared in England, is more pleasant to the taste.

The lesser stomach of buffalo, moose, or deer, is usually eaten raw and is very good; but that of the moose must be well washed, for its contents are rather bitter. The kidneys of moose and buffalo are usually eaten raw by the Southern Indians, and no sooner is one of these beasts killed than the hunter rips up the belly, thrusts in his arm, snatches out the kidneys, and eats them warm before the animal is quite dead. They also, at times, put their mouths to the wounds they have made and suck the blood, which, they say, quenches the thirst and is very nourishing.

After regaling ourselves plentifully and taking some rest, for it was almost impossible to sleep because of the mosquitoes, we once more set forward and, after walking about ten miles, arrived at that long-wished-for-spot – the Coppermine River.

Nine

I WAS SURPRISED to find the river so different from the description of it which the Indians had given at the Factory. Instead of being so large as to be navigable for shipping, as it had been represented by them, it was at this part scarcely navigable for an Indian canoe, being no more than 180 yards wide, full of shoals, and with three falls in sight at the first view.

Near the water's edge there is some wood, but not one tree grows on or near the tops of the hills between which the river runs. There appears to have been formerly a much greater quantity, but the trees seem to have been set on fire some years ago, and there are now ten dead trees for every living one. The whole timber appears to have been so crooked and dwarfish a growth, even in its greatest prosperity, as to be of little use for anything except firewood.

Soon after our arrival, three Indians were sent off as spies in order to see if any Eskimos were inhabiting the river-side between us and the sea. We followed more slowly, and after three-quarters of a mile we put up while most of the Indians went hunting and killed several musk-oxen and some deer. They were employed the rest of the day and night in splitting and drying the meat by the fire.

As we were not then in want of provisions, and as deer and other animals were plentiful, I was at a loss to account for this unusual economy on the part of my companions. However, I was soon informed that these precautions were made with a view to having ready-cooked victuals to serve us to the river's mouth, without being obliged to fire guns, or make the smoke of fires, and so alarm the natives if any should be at hand.

We set out again on the morning of the 15th of July, and I began a survey of the river, which I continued for about ten miles, until a heavy rain obliged us to put up. We lay that night at the northern extremity of the woods, the space before us to the sea being entirely barren hills and wide open marshes. In the course of the day I found the river full of shoals, and in places so diminished in width that it formed two more capital falls.

The weather being more pleasant the next day, I proceeded with my survey for another ten miles, but still found the river the same as before, being everywhere full of shoals and rapids.

About noon the three spies returned, and reported that five tents of Eskimos were on the west side of the river. They said also that the situation was very convenient for surprising them, and that they were only twelve miles from us.

The Indians would now pay no further attention to my survey, but were immediately engaged in planning how they might steal up on the poor Eskimos in the night, and kill them all while they slept. To accomplish this bloody design more effectively, the Indians thought it necessary to cross the river as soon as possible. Accordingly, after they had put their guns, spears and shields into good order, we made the crossing.

Upon our arrival on the west side, each man painted the front of his shield; some with the image of the sun, others with the moon, others with different kinds of birds and beasts of prey, and still others, with the images of imaginary beings which, according to their silly notions, are the inhabitants of the different elements of Earth, Sea and Air.

When I inquired their reasons for doing this, I was told that each man painted his shield with the image of the being on which he most relied for success in the intended battle. Some were content with a single representation, while others, doubtful I suppose of the power of any single one, covered their shields to the very margins with groups of hieroglyphics which were quite unintelligible to everyone except the painter.

When this piece of superstition was completed, we began to advance toward the Eskimo camp. Since we were careful to avoid crossing any hills, the distance was made much greater and, for the sake of keeping to the low ground, we were forced to walk through entire swamps of stiff, marly clay, sometimes up to the knees. However, our course, though very serpentine, was not so remote from the river as to exclude me from a view of it, and I was able to convince myself that it was just as unnavigable as the parts I had surveyed.

It is worth remarking that my crew, though an undisciplined rabble, and by no means accustomed to war or to command, seemingly acted, on this horrid occasion, with the utmost uniformity of sentiment. All were united in the general cause, and ready to follow Matonabbee, who had taken the lead, in accord with the advice of an old Copper Indian who had joined us on our first arrival at the river.

For once, reciprocity of interest was in general high regard amongst these people and no one was in want of anything that another could spare. Property of every kind that could be of use now ceased to be private, and those with more than they needed seemed proud to lend or give the surplus to those who were most in need.

The number of my crew was so much greater than what the five tents could contain, and the warlike manner in which the Indians were equipped was so superior to what could be expected of the poor Eskimos, that no less than a total massacre seemed likely to be the result, unless Providence should work a miracle for their deliverance.

The land was so situated that we walked under cover of hills and rocks till we were two hundred yards from the tents. There we lay in ambush for some time, watching the movements of the Eskimos; and here the Indians would have advised me to stay until the fight was over. To this plan I could by no means consent for I considered that, when the Eskimos came to be surprised, they would try every way to escape and, if they found me alone, not knowing me from an enemy, they would probably proceed to violence against me when no person was near me to assist.

For this reason I determined to accompany the Indians, telling them at the same time that I would not have any hand in the murder they were about to commit, unless I found it necessary for my own safety.

The Indians were not displeased with this proposal. One of them immediately fixed me a spear. Another lent me a broad bayonet for my protection, but it was too late to provide me with a target, nor did I want to be encumbered with such an unnecessary piece of lumber.

While we lay in ambush, the Indians performed the last minute ceremonies which were thought necessary before the engagement. These consisted chiefly of painting their faces; some all black, some all red, and some with a mixture of the two. To prevent their hair blowing in their eyes, it was either tied before and behind on both sides, or else cut off short all around. The next thing they considered was to make themselves as light as possible for running, which they did by pulling off their stockings, and either cutting off the sleeves of their jackets or rolling them up close to their armpits. Though the mosquitoes were so numerous as to surpass all credibility, yet some of the Indians actually pulled off their jackets and prepared to enter the lists quite naked, except for their breech-clouts and moccasins.

Fearing that I might have occasion to run with the rest, I also thought it advisable to pull off my stockings and cap, and to tie my hair as close as possible.

By the time the Indians had made themselves thus completely frightful, it was near one o'clock in the morning of the 17th. Finding all the Eskimos now quiet in their tents, the Indians chose this moment to attack. They rushed forth from their ambuscade, unperceived by the poor unsuspecting creatures until they were close to the very eaves of the tents. And so began the bloody slaughter, while I stood neuter in the rear.

The horrible scene was shocking beyond description. The unhappy victims had been surprised in the midst of their sleep, and had neither time nor power to make any resistance. Men, women and children, numbering upwards of twenty, ran stark naked from the tents and endeavoured to make good their escape; but the Indians having possession of all the landside, there was no place they could fly for shelter. The only alternative was to leap into the river; as none of them attempted it, they all fell victim to Indian barbarity.

The shrieks and groans of the poor expiring victims were truly dreadful. My horror was much increased at seeing a young girl of about eighteen years attacked so near me that, when the first spear was thrust into her side, she fell at my feet and twisted herself around my legs, so that it was with difficulty I could disengage myself from her dying grasp. Two Indian men were pursuing this unfortunate victim, and I solicited very hard for her life. The murderers made no reply until they had stuck both their spears through her body and transfixed her to the ground. They then looked me sternly in the face and began to ridicule me by asking if I desired an Eskimo wife; meanwhile paying not the slightest heed to the shrieks and agony of the poor wretch who was still twining around their spears like an eel.

Indeed, after receiving much abuse from them, I was at length obliged to desire only that they would be more expeditious in dispatching their victim out of her misery; otherwise I should be obliged, out of pity, to assist in the friendly office of putting an end to a fellow creature who had been so cruelly wounded.

On this request being made, one of the Indians hastily drew his spear from the place where it was first lodged, and pierced it through her breast near the heart. The love of life, however, even in this most miserable state, was so predominant that though this might justly be called the most merciful act that could be done for the poor creature, it still seemed to be unwelcome. Though much exhausted by pain and loss of blood, she made several efforts to ward off this friendly blow.

My situation, and the terror of my mind at beholding this butchery, cannot easily be conceived, much less described; and though I summed up all the fortitude which I was master of on the occasion, it was with difficulty that I could refrain from tears. I am confident that my features must have feelingly expressed how sincerely I was affected by this barbarous scene. Even at this hour I cannot reflect on the transactions of that horrid day without shedding tears.

The brutish manner in which these savages used the bodies that had been so cruelly bereaved of life was so shocking that it would be indecent to describe it, particularly their curiosity in examining, and the remarks they made on, the formation of the women; which, they pretended to say, differed materially from their own. For my own part I must acknowledge that however favourable the opportunity for determining that point might have been, yet my thoughts at the time were too much agitated to admit of any such remarks; and I firmly believe that had there actually been as much difference between them as there is said to be between the Hottentots and those of Europe, it would not have been in my power to have marked the distinction. I have reason to think, however, that there is no ground for the assertion, and I really believe that the declaration of the Indians on this occasion was utterly devoid of truth and proceeded only from the implacable hatred they bore to the whole tribe of people of whom I am speaking.

After the Indians had completed the murder of the poor Eskimos, seven other tents on the east side of the river immediately engaged their attention. Luckily for their inhabitants, our canoes and baggage had been left at some distance up the river, so that there was no means of getting across. However, the river was little more than eighty yards wide at his point, and the Indians began firing at the Eskimos. The poor Eskimos, though all up in arms, did not attempt to abandon their tents. In fact they were so unacquainted with firearms that, when the bullets struck the ground, they ran in crowds to see what was sent to them. At length one of the Eskimo men was shot in the calf of the leg, which put them in great confusion. They all immediately embarked in their kayaks and paddled to a shoal in the middle of the river which, being more than a gunshot from any part of the shore, put them out of the reach of our barbarians.

The Indians now began to plunder the tents of the deceased of all the copper utensils they could find, such as hatchets, bayonets, and knives. Afterwards they assembled on top of an adjacent high hill and, standing all in a cluster so as to form a solid circle, with their spears erect, gave many shouts of victory, while constantly clashing their spears against each other and calling out *"Tima! Tima!"* (which is to say, Friend, Friend!) by way of derision to the surviving Eskimos who were standing on the shoal almost knee-deep in water.

After parading the hill for some time, it was agreed to return up the river to the place where we had left our canoes and baggage, and then to cross the river again and plunder the tents on the east side. This resolution was immediately put in force, but, as ferrying across with only three canoes took a considerable time, several of the poor surviving Eskimos, probably thinking we had gone about our business, had meanwhile returned from the shoal to their habitations.

When we approached their tents, which we did under the cover of the rocks, we found them busily employed tying up bundles. These the Indians seized upon with

their usual ferocity, and the Eskimos immediately embarked. All of them got safe to the shoal except an old
man who was so intent on collecting his things that the
Indians came upon him before he could reach his kayak
and he fell a sacrifice to their fury. I verily believe that
not less than twenty had a hand in his death, as his whole
body was like a sieve.

I ought to have mentioned in its proper place that, in
returning for the canoes, we saw an old woman sitting by
the side of the water killing salmon, which lay at the foot
of the fall as thick as a shoal of herrings. Whether from
the noise of the fall, or a natural defect in the old
woman's hearing, she had no knowledge of the tragical
scene which had so lately been transacted at the tents.
When we first perceived her, she seemed perfectly at ease,
and was entirely surrounded with the produce of her
labour. From her behaviour, and from the appearance of
her eyes, which were as red as blood, it is probable that
her sight was not very good, for she scarcely discerned
that the Indians were her enemies till they were within
two spear-lengths of her.

It was then in vain that she attempted to fly, for the
wretches of my crew transfixed her to the ground in a few
seconds, and butchered her in the most savage manner.
There was scarcely a man among them who had not a
thrust at her with his spear. Many, in doing this, aimed at
torture rather than immediate death, as they not only
poked out her eyes, but stabbed her in many parts very
remote from those which are vital.

It may appear strange that a person supposed to be
almost blind should be employed at fishing, with any
degree of success; but when the multitude of fish is taken
into account, the wonder ceases. The fish were so
numerous at the foot of the fall that, when a light pole
armed with a few spikes (which was the instrument the
old woman had been using) was put under the water and
hauled up with a jerk, it was scarcely possible to miss

them. The numbers at this place were perhaps equal to anything that is related of the salmon at Kamchatka, or any other part of the world.

When the Indians had plundered the seven tents of all the copper utensils – which seemed the only things worth their notice – they threw all the tents and tent poles into the river, destroyed a vast quantity of dried salmon, musk-oxen flesh and other provisions, broke all the stone kettles and, in fact, did all the mischief they possibly could to distress the poor creatures they could not murder, and who were still standing on the shoal afore-mentioned, obliged to be woeful spectators of their great and perhaps irreparable loss.

After the Indians had completed this piece of wantonness, we sat down and made a good meal of fresh salmon. When we had finished our meal, which was the first we had enjoyed in many hours, the Indians told me they were again ready to assist me in making an end to my survey.

It was then five o'clock in the morning of the 17th and the sea was in sight about eight miles distant. I therefore instantly commenced my survey and pursued it to the mouth of the river, which I found all the way so full of shoals and rapids that it was not navigable even for a boat, and that it emptied itself into the sea over a ridge or bar. The tide was out, but I judged from the marks I saw on the edge of the ice that it flowed about twelve or four-teen feet, which will only reach a little way into the river's mouth. Here the sea is full of islands and shoals, as far as I could see with the assistance of a good pocket telescope. The sea ice was not then broken up, but was melted away for a distance of three-quarters of a mile from the main shore, and to a little distance round the islands and shoals. Having completed my survey, I erected a mark and took possession of the coast, which I was the first white man ever to see, on behalf of the Hudson's Bay Company.

We were now ready to return, but before continuing

with my narrative it may be fitting to give a brief account of the habits and customs of the Eskimos.

When I first entered the employment of the Hudson's Bay Company, it was as Mate of one of their sloops which was employed in trading with the Eskimos. I had, therefore, frequent opportunities of observing the miserable manner in which these people live.

In the course of our trade with them, we frequently purchased seal-skin bags, which we supposed to be full of oil. On opening them we sometimes found great quantities of venison, seals, and walrus paws, as well as salmon. As these were of no use to us, we gave them back to the Eskimos, who eagerly devoured them, though some of the articles had been perhaps a whole year in that state. They seemed to exult greatly at having so overreached us in the way of trade as to have sometimes a third of their bargain returned.

This method of preserving food, though it effectually guards it from the external air and from the flies, does not prevent putrefaction entirely, though it renders its progress very slow. Pure seal or walrus oil is of such a quality that it never freezes in the coldest winter, which is a happy circumstance for people condemned to live in this most rigorous climate.

While these magazines last, they have nothing more to do when hunger assails them but to open one of the bags, take out a side of venison, a few seals, walrus paws, or some half-rotted salmon and, without any preparation, sit down and make a meal. The lake or river beside which they pitch their tent affords them water, which is their constant drink.

Besides this extraordinary food already mentioned, they have several other dishes equally disgusting to the European palate. I will only mention one, which is made of the raw liver of a deer cut in small pieces and mixed with the contents of the stomach of the same animal. The further the digestion of these contents has already taken place, the better it suits their taste. I have also seen them eat whole handfuls of maggots which were produced in meat by blow-flies, and it is their constant custom, when their noses bleed by accident, to lick the blood into their mouths and swallow it.

But if we consider the inhospitable part of the globe they are destined to inhabit, and the great distress to which they are frequently driven by hunger, we shall no longer be surprised at finding they can relish anything, but rather admire the wisdom and kindness of Providence in forming the palates and powers of all creatures in such a manner as is best adapted to the food, climate, and other circumstances of their respective situations.

It is no less true that these people, when I first knew them, would not eat any of our provisions. Though some would taste our sugar, raisins, figs, and bread, they soon spit it out again with evident marks of distaste; so they had no greater relish for our food, than we had for theirs. At present the Eskimos about Churchill River will eat any part of our provisions and will drink a draught of porter or a little brandy and water. They are now so far civilized, and attached to the English, that I am persuaded any of the Company's servants who could habituate themselves to their diet and manner of life, might now live quite secure under their protection. They live in a state of perfect freedom, none claiming the superiority over, or acknowledging the least subordination to another, except what is due from children to their parents.

Ten

HAVING finished our business at the river, we set out to visit the copper mines themselves; but after walking about twelve miles south by east, we stopped and took a little sleep. This was the first time any of us had closed his eyes since the 15th, and it was now six o'clock in the morning of the 18th. The Indians killed a musk-ox, but as we had nothing but wet moss for fuel, and so could not have a fire, we were obliged to eat the meat raw, and found it intolerable, as it happened to be an old beast.

It may not be improper here to give some further account of the river, and the country adjacent, with its productions, and those who inhabit its dreary regions.

Apart from the stunted trees already mentioned, there is plenty of the plant known as Labrador Tea, some low plants the natives use for tobacco, and a few cranberry and other berry bushes. The woods themselves gradually grow thinner and smaller as they approach the sea, and the last little tuft of pines I saw was about thirty miles from the river mouth.

The general course of the river is about north by east, but in some places it is very crooked. Its breadth varies from twenty yards to four or five hundred. The banks are, in general, of solid rock, both sides of which correspond so exactly as to leave no doubt that the channel of the river has been caused by some terrible convulsion of nature. Some of the Indians say that this river takes its rise from the north-west side of Large White Stone Lake, which is at the distance of nearly three hundred miles in a straight line. From the falls where my Indians killed the Eskimos, and which I have distinguished by the name of Bloody Falls, it is about eight miles to the sea-side.

The Eskimos at this river are but low in stature, none exceeding middle size and, though broad set, are neither well made nor strong bodied. Their complexion is of a dirty copper colour, although some of the women are more fair and ruddy. Their dress much resembles that of the Greenlanders in Davis Straits, except for the women's boots, which are not stiffened out with whalebone; and the tails of their jackets, which are not more than a foot long.

Their arms and fishing tackle are bows and arrows, spears, lances and darts, which, for want of good edge-tools, are inferior to those of the Greenlanders. Their arrows are either shod with a triangular piece of black stone like slate or, less commonly, with a piece of copper.

The body of their kayaks is on the same construction as that of other Eskimos, but these, like their arms, are by no means so neat as those I have seen in Hudson's Bay.

The tents are made of parchment deer-skins with the hair remaining on them, and are pitched in the circular form. But these are undoubtedly no more than summer habitations, for I saw the remains of two miserable hovels which, from the situation, the structure, and the vast quantities of bones and other rubbish lying near them, had certainly been some of their winter retreats. These houses were placed on the south side of a hill, and one half of each was underground, while the upper parts were closely set around with poles in a conical form. When inhabited, they are undoubtedly covered with skins and banked around with snow. They could not contain more than six or eight people each, and even that number would find them but miserable habitations.

The household furniture consists of stone kettles or

pots, and wooden troughs of various sizes, with dishes, scoops and spoons made of musk-ox horns. The pots are carved of a pepper-and-salt stone which appears to be very porous, but is nevertheless perfectly tight and will sound as clear a note as a china bowl. Some of these pots are large enough to contain five or six gallons. It is impossible that these poor people can perform this arduous work with anything other than harder stones as tools, yet these kettles are far superior to any I ever saw on Hudson's Bay, every one being ornamented with neat mouldings around the rim, and some of the large ones with a kind of flute-work at the corners. In shape they are a long square, somewhat wider at the top than at the bottom. Strong handles of stone are left at each end to lift them up.

The hatchets of these people are made of a thick lump of native copper about five or six inches long, bevelled away at one end like a chisel. This is lashed into the end of a piece of wood in such a manner as to form a kind of adze. It is applied to the material being worked, like a chisel, and driven in with a heavy club, for neither the weight of the tool, nor the sharpness of the metal, will allow it to be handled as we would use an adze or axe.

The men's bayonets, and the women's knives, are also made of copper, the former being shaped like the ace of spades, with handles of deer horn a foot long.

Among all the spoils of the twelve tents, only two small pieces of iron were found, both of which had been made into knife blades.

These people had a numerous and fine breed of dogs with sharp erect ears, sharp noses, and bushy tails. Though they were all tethered to stones, I do not recall that my companions killed or hurt one of these animals; but after we left the tents they wished they had taken some of these fine dogs with them.

Though these people are in many ways similar to those of Hudson's Bay, yet there is one unusual custom which prevails amongst them; namely that of the men having all the hairs of their heads pulled out by the roots. The women, however, wore their hair at full length.

There are many birds about the place, particularly by the sea-side; and musk-oxen, deer, grizzled bears, Alpine hares, white owls, ravens, partridges, ground-squirrels, common squirrels, ermines and mice, are the constant inhabitants. In many places, by the sides of the hills where the snow lay to a great depth, the dung of the musk-ox and deer lay in such long and continuous heaps as to point to these places being much frequented paths during the winter. It is perhaps not generally known, even to the curious, that the dung of the musk-ox, though from so large an animal, is so near the shape, size, and colour of that of the Alpine hare as to be very difficult to distinguish, except by the quantity.

We also saw the "Alarm Bird," or "Bird of Warning," as the Copper Indians call it, which is of the owl genus. When it perceives any people, or a beast, it hovers over them for a time, making a loud screaming noise like the crying of a child. In this manner they are said sometimes to follow passengers for a whole day. The Copper Indians put great confidence in these birds, who frequently apprise them of the approach of strangers or of the whereabouts of herds of musk-oxen or deer. The Eskimos do not seem to have the same opinion of these birds, since all the time the Indians lay in ambush a large flock was continually flying about, hovering alternately over the tents, and then the Indians, and making a noise sufficient to wake any man out of a sound rest.

After a sleep of five or six hours we once more set out and walked eighteen miles to the south-south-east, when we arrived at one of the copper mines, which lies twenty-nine or thirty miles distant from the river mouth.

The mine, if it deserves that appellation, is no more than an entire jumble of rocks and gravel which has been rent many ways by an earthquake. Through the ruins there runs a small river. The Indians had represented this mine as so rich and valuable that, if a Factory were built at the river, a ship might be ballasted with the ore with the same ease and dispatch as is done with stones at Churchill River. By their account the hills were entirely composed of copper, all in handy lumps, like a heap of pebbles.

Their account differed so much from the truth that I, and all my companions, expended near four hours in search of some of the metal, with such poor success that only one piece of any size could be found. This, however, was remarkably good, and weighed above four pounds.

The Indians imagine that every bit of copper they find resembles some object in nature but, from what I saw, it requires a great share of invention to make this out. Different people had different ideas on the subject, for the large piece of copper had not been long found before it had twenty different names, although at last it was generally allowed to resemble an Alpine hare couchant. The Indians consider the largest pieces, with the least dross and the fewest branches, are best for their use; as by the help of fire and two stones they can beat it into any shape they wish.

Before Churchill River was settled by the Hudson's Bay Company some fifty years previously, the Northern Indians had no other metal but copper, except a small quantity of ironwork which a party who had visited York Factory about 1714 had purchased, and some pieces of old iron left at Churchill River by Captain Monk. This being the case, numbers of them from all quarters used to resort to these hills every summer in search of copper, from which they made hatchets, ice-chisels, bayonets, knives, awls, arrow-heads, etc. The many paths which had been beaten by the Indians on these occasions are yet perfect in many places, especially on the dry ridges and hills.

The Copper Indians set a great value on their native

metal even to this day, and prefer it to iron for almost every use except that of hatchet, knife and awl. There is a strange tradition amongst them that the first person to discover these mines was a woman. For several years she conducted them to this place, but as she was the only woman in the company, some of the men took such liberties with her that she vowed revenge on them. She was a great conjurer, and when the men loaded themselves with copper and were going to return to their homes, she refused to accompany them. She said that she would sit on the mine until she sank into the ground, and the copper would sink with her. The next year, when the men went for more copper, they found her sunk to the waist, though still alive; and the quantity of copper had much decreased. The year following, she had quite disappeared, and all the principal parts of the mine with her. After that, nothing remained on the surface but a few small pieces scattered at a great distance from each other.

The Copper Indians no longer barter much copper to the Northern Indians, as they were wont to do, but now barter fur instead. The established rule is that everything brought from Churchill River shall be sold to them at ten times the price paid for it by the Northern Indians. Thus a hatchet, bought at the Factory for one beaver-skin, is sold to these people at the advanced price of one thousand per cent. For a small brass kettle they pay sixty marten, or twenty beaver in other kinds of fur.

What is meant by "beaver in other kinds of fur" must be understood as follows: For the easier trading with the Indians, the Hudson's Bay Company have made a full-grown beaver skin the standard by which they rate all other furs. Thus, some valuable kinds of fur are rated at four beaver each, while those of very inferior value may be rated at twenty to make one beaver skin. It is thus that the term "Made Beaver" as a standard of exchange is to be understood.

Our carrier Indians used to purchase most of the furs they brought to the Company's Factory from these Copper Indians, and from their neighbours the Dog-ribbed Indians who live even farther to the west. The reason for this was that there were few furs in the Northern Indian country, and since they were at war with the Athapuscow Indians they were prevented from penetrating far enough southward to meet with many animals of the fur kind. So the deer-skins and furs they could extort from the Copper and Dog-ribbed Indians composed the whole of their trade which, until very lately, seldom if ever exceeded six thousand Made Beaver per annum.

At the time this journal was written, the peace with the Southern Indians had redounded greatly to the advantage of our Northern Indians, and of the Company. The good effect of this harmony increased the trade from that quarter to the amount of eleven thousand Made Beaver per annum. In addition to the advantage which arose to the Company, the Northern Indians reaped innumerable benefits from having access to the fine and plentiful country of the Athapuscow Indians.

However, though it is no part of the record of my journey, I must here carry forward in time and interject a tragic addition to the account of the ultimate results of the peace between the Northern and the Southern Indians.

Some years after my journey was concluded, the Northern Indians, by visiting their Southern friends, contracted the smallpox from them. In a few years this disease carried off nine-tenths of them; and particularly those who composed the trade at Churchill Factory. The few survivors afterwards followed the example of the Athapuscow tribe, and traded with the Canadians who were then becoming established in the country of those Indians.

Thus it is that a very few years have proved my short-sightedness; for it would really have been much more to the advantage of the Company, as well as having prevented the depopulation of the Northern Indian country, if they had still remained at war with the Southern Indians. At the same time it is impossible now to say what increase in trade might not have risen in time from a constant and regular traffic with the Copper and Dog-ribbed peoples. But these, having been cut off from our Factory by the decimation of the Northern Indians, soon sank into their original barbarism, and a war ensued between the two tribes for the sake of a few remnants of ironwork that was left amongst them; with the result that almost the whole Copper Indian race was destroyed.

Before the time of my journey, and for a short while afterwards, several attempts had been made to induce the Copper and Dog-ribbed Indians to visit the Company Fort at Churchill River. For that purpose many presents were sent; but the attempts were never attended with success. Though several Copper Indians visited the Fort in the capacity of servants of the Northern Indians, and though these were sent back loaded with presents for their countrymen, yet the Northern Indians always plundered them of the whole, soon after they left the Fort.

This treatment was undoubtedly a political scheme of the carrier Indians to prevent direct intercourse, which would have greatly lessened their consequence and emolument. However, superstition was also a lasting barrier against these people having settled communication with the Factory, as few of them chose to travel in countries so remote from their own, under the pretence that the change of air and provisions was highly prejudicial to their health, and that not one of three who ever undertook the journey lived to return. The first of these reasons was no more than gross superstition, but the latter was only too true, owing to the treachery and cruelty of the Northern Indians.

Not long before my journey began, Captain Keelshies took twelve of these people under his charge, all heavy laden with the most valuable furs. But even before they had got to the Fort, Captain Keelshies and his crew had got all their furs from them on payment of provisions for their support; and had then obliged them to continue to carry the furs, on the Northern Indians' account.

On their arrival at the Fort, Keelshies laid claim to much merit for having brought these richly laden strangers to the Factory, and assured the Governor that he might expect a great increase in trade as a result of Keelshies' interest and assiduity. One of the strangers was therefore dubbed Captain, and treated accordingly while at the Fort and, on his departure, he and his countrymen were loaded with presents.

There seemed to be great propriety in the Governor's conduct in the matter, but however well-intended, it had quite the contrary effect. Keelshies and the rest of his execrable gang, not content with sharing the profits of all the furs, determined to get all the gifts given these poor people by the Governor, as well.

As they did not have the courage to kill the Copper Indians outright, they arranged a deep-laid scheme for their destruction by marooning them on an island. Having stripped them, they went off, leaving the unfortunate people to perish from want. On my return journey to the Fort, I saw the bones of these poor people; but it was not made known to the Governor for some years afterwards for fear of prejudicing him against Captain Keelshies.

A similar incident nearly happened to a Copper Indian who accompanied me on that same journey for, after we had all ferried across the Seal River, and the poor man's bundle had been brought across, he himself was left alone on the opposite shore. Only Matonabbee would go for him. The wind blew so hard that Matonabbee stripped himself naked, to be ready for swimming, but he soon brought the Indian safely over in the canoe, to the no small mortification of those who had charge of him.

On their return from the Factory to the west, this man put himself under Matonabbee's protection, and in due course Matonabbee delivered him in good health to his father, with all his goods intact.

Eleven

WE NOW PROCEEDED at a very great pace to the south-eastward to rejoin the people we had left, and after six days of travel, during one of which we walked forty-two miles, we arrived at Congecathawhachaga.

To our great disappointment we found that our women had departed, so that when we arrived not an Indian was to be found except an old man, and his family, who had arrived in our absence and was waiting at the crossing-place with some furs for Matonabbee. This old man, who was the Leader's father-in-law, had another of his daughters with him which he offered to the great man; but she was not accepted.

Our stay was of very short duration for, on seeing a smoke to the southward, we immediately crossed the river and walked toward it. We found it to be burning moss which had been fired by our women; but they had departed. Although the afternoon was far advanced, we pursued them. We had not gone far before we saw another smoke at a great distance, toward which we shaped our course; but notwithstanding that we redoubled our pace, it was eleven o'clock at night before we reached it. To our great mortification we found it to be the place where the women had slept the night before.

The Indians, finding that their wives were so near as to be within one ordinary day's walk, determined not to rest until they had joined them. Accordingly we pursued our course and, about two o'clock in the morning of the 25th of July, we came up with some of the women who had pitched their tents by the side of Cogead Lake.

Since leaving Coppermine we had travelled so hard, and had taken so little rest, that my feet had swelled considerably and I had become quite stiff at the ankles. I had so little power to direct my feet, when walking, that I frequently knocked them against the stones with such force as not only to jar and disorder them, but my legs also. The nails of my toes were bruised to such a degree that several of them festered and dropped off. To add to this mishap, the skin was entirely chafed from the tops of both feet and from between every toe. The sand and gravel, which I could by no means exclude, irritated the raw parts so much that, for a day before we arrived at the women's tents, I left the print of my feet in blood with every step. Several of the Indians complained that their feet also were sore; but not one of them was in so bad a state as mine.

This being the first time I had seen anyone footfoundered, I was in great apprehension for the consequences. Though I was but little fatigued in body, yet the excruciating pain suffered in walking had such an effect on my spirits that, if the Indians had continued to travel two or three days longer at that unmerciful rate, I must unavoidably have been left behind, for my feet were quite honeycombed by the dirt and gravel eating into the raw flesh.

As soon as we arrived at the tents, I washed and cleaned my feet in warm water, then bathed the swelled parts with spirits of wine and dressed the raw places with Turner's cerate. As we did not move on the following day, the swelling abated and the raw parts were not so much inflamed.

Rest, though essential to my recovery, could not be procured, for the Indians were desirous of joining the remainder of their wives and families as soon as possible. Consequently they would not stop even a day, so that on the 27th we again began to move. Though they now travelled only eight or nine miles a day, it was with the utmost difficulty that I could follow them. Fortunately the weather proved fine and pleasant, and the ground was, in general, pretty dry and free from stones.

On July 31st we arrived at the place where the wives and children left behind at Peshew Lake were to have joined us on our return from the Coppermine River. Here we found several tents of Indians, but these belonged to Matonabbee and some few others, and the rest of the women had not yet arrived. However, we saw a large smoke to the eastward, which we guessed might be the missing people. Accordingly the next morning Matonabbee dispatched some of his young men in quest of them, and on the 5th of August they joined us. Contrary to expectations, a great number of other Indians were with them, to the amount of more than forty tents.

Among these Indians was the man Matonabbee had stabbed when we were at Clowey. Now, with the greatest submission, he led his wife to the Leader's tent, set her down by his side, and retired without saying a word.

Matonabbee took no notice of her, though she was bathed in tears. By degrees, after reclining herself on her elbow for a time, she lay down, sobbing, and said: *"See'd dinne! See'd dinne!"* which is, "My husband! My husband!"

On hearing this, Matonabbee told her that if she had respected him as such she would not have run away from him, and that now she was at liberty to go where she pleased. On which she got up with seeming reluctance, though most assuredly with a light heart, and returned to her former husband's tent.

Several of the Indians at this camp being very ill, the conjurers, who are always the doctors, and who pretend to perform great cures, began to try their skill.

The chief disorders which afflict these people are a scorbutic ailment, consumptions, and the flux. The first of these, though troublesome, is never known to prove fatal unless accompanied by some inward complaint. However, the two latter diseases carry off great numbers of both sexes and all ages. Indeed few of them live to any great age, perhaps owing to the great fatigue they undergo from their youth upwards in procuring a subsistence for themselves and their offspring.

Though the scorbutic disorder appears to be infectious, and it is rare to see one have it without the whole tent's crew being affected by it, this is not proof, by any means, that it *is* contagious. I rather attribute it to the effects of bad water, or the unwholesomeness of the fish they catch in particular places. Were it otherwise, a single family would, in a short time, communicate it to the whole tribe; but on the contrary this disease is never known to spread.

It attacks the hands and feet, not sparing the soles and palms, of the younger people. Those of riper years generally have it about the wrists, insteps and posteriors; and, particularly in the latter, the blotches, or boils, as they may be justly called, are often as large as the top of a man's thumb. This disorder most frequently makes its appearance in the summer when the Indians are out on the barren ground. Though it is not reckoned dangerous, yet it is so obstinate as not to yield to any medicine that has ever been applied to it at the Company's factories.

Here it is necessary to remark that the Indians themselves use no medicine, either for internal or external complaints, but perform all their cures by charms. In ordinary cases, sucking the afflicted part, blowing and singing into it, hawking and spitting, and at the same time uttering a heap of unintelligible jargon, compose the whole process of the cure.

For some inward complaints, such as griping in the intestines and difficulty of making water, it is very common to see those jugglers blowing into the anus, or into the parts adjacent, till their eyes are almost starting out of their heads. The operation is performed indifferently on all, without regard either to age or sex. The accumulation of so large a quantity of wind is, at times, apt to occasion some extraordinary emotions, which are not easily suppressed by the sick person. As there is no vent for it but the channel by which it was conveyed thither, it sometimes occasions an odd scene between the doctor and his patient. I once wantonly called this an "engagement"; for which I was later exceedingly sorry, as it highly offended several of the Indians, particularly the juggler and the sick person, both of whom were men I much esteemed. Except in that moment of levity, it had ever been no less my inclination than my interest to show every respect to them.

I have often admired the great pains the jugglers take to deceive their credulous countrymen, while at the same time they are industrious and persevering in their efforts to relieve them. When a friend for whom they have a particular regard is, as they suppose, dangerously ill, they have recourse to another very extraordinary piece of superstition. This is no less than pretending to swallow hatchets, ice-chisels, or broad bayonets and knives, out of a notion that undertaking such desperate feats will have some influence in appeasing death.

On such occasions a conjuring house is erected, in the shape of a small square tent, with no vacancy left to admit the light. The patient is carried into the middle of the tent, accompanied by the conjurer, or conjurers, sometimes five or six in number. Before they enter, they strip themselves quite naked, then they kneel around the sick person and blow at the parts affected.

The door is kept shut, but behind it they are heard to sing and talk as if conversing with familiar spirits which, they say, appear to them in the shape of beasts and birds of prey.

When they have had a sufficient conference with these necessary agents, they ask for the hatchet or bayonet, which is always prepared by another person who fastens a long string to the haft. This is for the convenience of hauling it up again after they have swallowed it, for they admit that iron and steel would be very difficult to digest. Besides, these tools are useful, and not easily to be procured, and it would be very ungenerous of the conjurers to digest them.

One man was so dangerously ill at our present camp that it was thought necessary that the conjurers should use some of these wonderful experiments. One of them thereupon consented to swallow a broad bayonet. After the preliminaries, which I have already described, were gone through, the conjurer advanced to the door and asked for the bayonet. The string had already been attached, together with a short piece of wood at the other end of the string to prevent him from swallowing it. I could not help observing that the length of the piece of wood was not more than the width of the bayonet; however, as it answered the purpose, it did as well as if it had been as long as a handspike.

Though I am not so credulous as to believe that the conjurer actually swallowed the bayonet, yet I must acknowledge that, in the twinkling of an eye, he conveyed it to – God knows where; and the small piece of wood, or one exactly like it, was confined close to his teeth.

He then paraded back and forward for a short time, when he feigned to be greatly disordered in his stomach and bowels, groaning most hideously, and putting his body into several distorted attitudes very suitable to the occasion. He then returned to the door of the hut and, after making many strong efforts to vomit, he produced the bayonet by the help of the string and apparently hauled it out of his mouth, to the no small surprise of all present. He then returned into the conjuring house where he continued his incantations, without intermission, for twenty-four hours.

Though I was not close to his elbow when he performed the feat, yet I thought myself near enough (and I can assure my readers that I was all attention) to have detected him. Indeed, I must confess that it appeared to me to be a very nice piece of deception, especially as it was performed by a man quite naked.

The sick man soon recovered; but, had he not done so, his body would have been left unburied as we passed on. These Indians never bury their dead, but always leave the bodies where they die, so that they are supposed to be devoured by beasts and birds of prey; for which reason the people will not eat foxes, ravens, wolves, etc., unless it be through necessity.

The death of a near relation affects them so much that they rend all their clothes from their backs and go naked until some person, less afflicted, relieves them. After the death of a close relative they mourn, as it may be called, for a whole year. These mournful periods are distinguished not by any particular dress but only by cutting off the hair; and the ceremony consists of almost perpetual crying. Even when walking they make an odd howling noise, often repeating the relationship of the deceased. When they reflect seriously on the loss of a good friend, it has such an effect upon them that they give uncommon loose to their grief.

They had a tradition among them that the first person upon earth was a woman who, after being some time alone, found an animal like a dog, which followed her to her cave and soon grew fond and domestic. This dog, they said, had the art of transforming itself into the shape of a handsome young man, which it frequently did at night. With the approach of day, however, it resumed its former shape, so that the woman looked on all that happened in the nights as dreams and delusions. But the transformations were productive of the same consequences which at present generally follow such intimate connections between the two sexes; and so the mother of the world began to advance in her pregnancy.

Not long after this happened, a man of such surprising height that his head reached up to the clouds, came to level the land; which at that time was a very rude mass. After he had done this, with the help of his walking-stick, he marked out the lakes, ponds and rivers, and immediately caused them to be filled with water.

He then took the dog, tore it to pieces, and threw the guts into the lakes and rivers, commanding them to become the different kinds of fish. The dog's flesh he dispersed over the land to become different kinds of beasts and land-animals. He also tore the skin into small pieces and threw it into the air, commanding it to become all kinds of birds. After this was done he gave the woman and her offspring full power to kill, eat, and never spare; for he had commanded the fish, birds, and beasts to multiply for her use, in abundance. After this injunction he returned to the place whence he came, and has not been heard of since.

Twelve

On the ninth of August we once more pursued our way, continuing in the south-west quarter. All the Indians who had been in our company, except twelve tents, struck off in different ways. As to myself, having had several days' rest, my feet were completely healed, though the skin remained very tender for some time.

From the 19th to the 25th we walked by the side of Large White Stone Lake, which is about forty miles long but of very unequal breadth. The river coursing from this lake is said to run a long way westward, and then trend north to form the main branch of the Coppermine River.

Deer were very plentiful the whole way, and the Indians killed great numbers of them daily, for the sake of their skins; for at this time of the year their pelts were in good season, and the hair was of a proper length for clothing.

The great destruction which is made of the deer in those parts, at this season of the year, is almost incredible. As they are never known to have more than one young at a time, it is wonderful that they do not become scarce; but so far is this from being the case that the eldest Northern Indian in all their tribe will affirm that the deer are as plentiful now as they have ever been. The scarcity or abundance of these animals in different places at the same season is caused, in a great measure, by the winds which prevail for some time before. The deer are supposed by the natives to walk always in the direction from which the wind blows, except when they migrate in search of the opposite sex, for the purpose of propagating their species.

It requires the prime parts of the skins from eight or ten deer to make a complete suit of warm clothing for a grown person during the winter. The skins should be taken in August or early September, for after that time the hair is not only too long, but is loose in the pelt, and will drop off at the slightest injury.

Besides these skins, which must retain their hair, each person requires several others to be dressed into leather for stockings and moccasins, and for light summer clothing. Several more are wanted to make thongs for their snowshoes, snares for deer, thongs for their sledges, and for any other use where strings or lines are needed. Therefore each person requires, in the course of a year, upward of twenty deerskins for clothing and domestic uses, let alone those which are needed for tents, sleeping bags, and many other things.

Skins that are taken after the rutting season are not only very thin, but also full of worms and warbles which render them of little value. Indeed the chief use of the hides taken in winter is for the purposes of food, and really, when the hair is properly taken off, and all the warbles are squeezed out, if they are then well boiled they are far from being disagreeable.

The Indians never could persuade me to eat the warble worms, of which some of them, and in particular the children, are remarkably fond. They are eaten raw and alive, and are said, by those who like them, to be as fine as gooseberries. But the idea of eating such things – many of which are as large as the first joint of the little finger – was sufficient to give me an unalterable disgust.

The type of clothing worn by these people makes them very subject to be lousy; but that is so far from being thought a disgrace that the best among them amuse themselves with catching and eating these vermin. They are so fond of this sport that the produce of a lousy head or garment affords them not only pleasing amusement, but a delicious repast. Matonabbee was so fond of these vermin that he frequently set five or six of his strapping wives to work to louse their hairy deer-skin shifts; the produce of which being always very considerable, he eagerly received it with both hands and licked them up as fast, and with as good a grace, as any European epicure would eat the mites in cheese.

However, when I acknowledge that the warbles out of the deer's back, and the domestic human lice, were the only things I ever saw my companions eat, of which I did not partake myself, I trust I shall not be reckoned over-delicate in my appetite.

The month of October is the rutting season for the deer, and after the courtship is over, the bucks separate from the does. The bucks proceed westward to take shelter in the woods during the winter, but the does remain out in the barren grounds the whole year. This, however, is not without exceptions, as I have frequently seen does in the woods.

The old bucks' horns are very large, with many branches, and always drop off in November, which is about the time they approach the woods. The does, however, do not shed their horns till summer.

The deer in the parts in which we were, are usually in motion from east to west, or west to east, according to the season or the prevailing winds. This is the principal reason why the Northern Indians are always shifting their station.

There is an old vulgar saying, generally received amongst the lower class of people in England, concerning the bucks shedding their yards, or more properly, the glands of their penis, yearly. Whether this be true in England or not, it is certainly not true in any of the countries bordering Hudson's Bay.

With equal truth I can assert, however, that the Alpine hare in Hudson's Bay actually undergoes something similar to what is vulgarly ascribed to the English deer. I have seen and handled several of them, killed just after they had coupled in the spring, with the penis dried up and shrivelled like the navel-string of young animals.

I have thought proper to give this remark a place in my journal because, in all probability, it is not generally known, even to those gentlemen who have made natural history their chief study. If their researches are of any benefit to mankind, it is to be regretted that Providence has made the greater part of them too secure from want to be obliged to travel for ocular proofs of what they assert in their publications. They are, therefore, wisely content to stay at home and enjoy the blessings with which they are endowed, resting satisfied to collect such information as they require from those who are necessitated to be travellers. It is true, and I am sorry to say it is so, that I come under the latter description. But I hope I have not, or shall not, advance anything in this journal that will not stand the test of experiment.

After leaving White Stone Lake, we continued our travels until the 3rd of September, when we arrived at a small river belonging to Point Lake. Here we were forced to remain for several days because of the boisterous weather which, with much rain, snow, and frost, prevented us from crossing the river in our small canoes.

On the 8th we came to a few small scrubby woods, which were the first we had seen from the 25th of May, except those we had perceived at the Coppermine River.

During our passage to this place, one of the Indians' wives, who for some time had been in a consumption, had become so weak as to be unable to travel. Amongst these people this is the most deplorable state to which a human being can possibly be brought. Whether she had been given over by the doctors, or whether it was from want of friends, no expedients were taken for her recovery so that, without much ceremony, she was left unassisted to perish above-ground.

Though this was the first instance of its kind I had seen, it is the common practice of these Indians. When a grown person is so ill, especially in the summer, as not to be able to walk, they say it is better to leave one who is past recovery than for the whole family to sit down and starve to death, without being able to assist the afflicted one. On these occasions the relations of the sick generally leave them some victuals and water and, if the situation affords it, some fuel. The person being left is also acquainted with the road the rest will follow. After covering the sick persons with deer-skins, the rest then take their leave and walk away crying.

Sometimes persons left thus will recover, and come up to their friends, or wander about till they meet with other Indians. Although instances of this kind are seldom known, yet the poor woman above-mentioned came up with us three several times. At length, poor creature, she dropped back for the last time.

A custom apparently so unnatural is, perhaps, not to be found among any other of the human race. If properly considered, however, it may with justice be ascribed to necessity and self-preservation rather than to the want of humanity. Necessity, added to a national custom, contributes to make scenes of this kind less shocking to those people than they must appear to the more civilized part of mankind.

The weather had now become very cold, with much snow and sleet, which seemed to promise an early winter. Since the deer were very plentiful, and there were here sufficient woods for fuel and tent poles, the Indians proposed that we encamp in order to make winter clothing, snowshoes and temporary sledges, and to prepare a large quantity of dried meat and fat to carry us forward. This seemed particularly necessary from the accounts of the Indians that they had always experienced a scarcity of every kind of game in the direction we proposed to go after leaving Point Lake.

The weather grew worse until, by the 30th of September, all the ponds and lakes were frozen over so hard that we were enabled to cross them on the ice without danger. October came in very roughly, attended by heavy falls of snow and much drift. On the night of the 6th, a heavy gale of wind put us in great disorder, for the few woods about did not furnish us with the least shelter from it. It overset several of the tents, and mine shared in the disaster; which I cannot sufficiently lament, for the butt-ends of the poles fell on my quadrant and broke it so that it was rendered completely useless. As it was no longer even worth the carriage, I gave the brass-work to the Indians, who cut it into small lumps and made use of it for ammunition.

On the 23rd of October, some Copper and Dog-ribbed Indians came to our tents to trade their furs. They made their purchases from us at a very extravagant price, for one of the Indians in my company got no less than forty beaver and sixty marten skins for one piece of iron which he had stolen when he was last at the Fort.

Another of the strangers had about forty beaver skins which he owed to Matonabbee because of an old debt; but one of the old Northern Indians seized this fur, notwithstanding that he knew it to be Matonabbee's property. This treatment, together with the other insults he had received, so annoyed the Leader that he now renewed his earlier resolution of leaving his own country and going to reside with the Athapuscow Indians.

As the objective of my journey had now been achieved, I did not try to influence him, either one way or the other. Indeed, by his conversations with the other Indians of our party, I soon understood that they all intended to make an excursion into the Athapuscow country in order to kill beaver and moose.

Fur animals of all sorts had been scarce during our journey, but the exceedingly small numbers of furs taken by our Indians was more probably due to their indolence. It is true that our moving so much from place to place did at times make the building of traps not worth while. However, if these people had taken advantage of the favourable opportunities, and if they had been possessed of half the industry of the Company's servants (the Southern Indians) in the vicinity of Hudson's Bay, they might with ease have caught many hundreds.

By October 30th, all our winter clothing, snowshoes, and temporary sledges being completed, we once more set out and walked to the southward for the next five days on the ice of a large lake. This lake, which I have called No Name, is about fifty miles long from north to south. It is said to abound in fine fish, but the weather was so cold when we crossed it that it was impossible to sit on the ice for any length of time to angle. Nevertheless, a few exceedingly fine trout and some large pike were caught by my companions.

Arriving at the south side of the lake, we shaped our course to the south-west and, though the weather was in general very cold, we every night found tufts of wood in which we could pitch our tents, and so were able to make some defence against the weather.

By the 10th of November we had reached the edge of the main forests, and here we paused to make proper sledges, after which we proceeded again to the south-west. Deer and all kinds of game were so scarce that nothing was killed by our company; however, we still had provisions which we had prepared during our stay at Point Lake.

On the 20th we arrived at Anaw'd Whoie, or Indian Lake, having crossed part of Methy Lake, and walked near eighty miles on the ice of a river belonging to it.

Anaw'd Lake, though so small as not to exceed twenty miles in breadth, is celebrated by the natives for abounding with fish during the winter. Accordingly, our Indians set all their nets, and met with such success that in ten days the roes alone were as much as the women could haul after them upon the sledges. The roes of the whitefish are particularly esteemed by the Indians, for two pounds of roe, well bruised, will make four gallons of thick broth and, if properly managed, will be as white as rice.

Rabbits were here so plentiful that several of the In-

dians snared twenty or thirty a night; and the spruce partridge were so numerous and tame that I have known an
Indian to kill twenty in a day with his bow and arrows.
Though the flesh of these birds is generally black and bitter, from their feeding on the brush of the fir trees, they
make a change of diet and are thought very good by the
natives, who are as fond of variety as any people. In fact
they will go to as great lengths to gratify their palates as
the greatest epicure in England. I have frequently known
Matonabbee and some other Indians to send young men
to kill a few partridge, at an expense of ammunition
which would have killed sufficient deer to maintain their
families for many days; whereas the partridges they got
were eaten in one meal. To heighten the luxury of such
occasions, the partridges are boiled in a kettle of sheer
fat, which renders them far finer flavoured than when
boiled in water or common broth. Deer-skins, boiled in
fat, are also exceedingly good eating.

During our stay at Anaw'd Lake, several of the Indians
were sickly, particularly one man who had been hauled
on a sledge by his brother for two months. His disorder
was the dead palsy, which totally affected one side of his
body. Besides this dreadful disorder, he had some inward
complaints and a total loss of appetite, so that he was
reduced to a mere skeleton, and was so weak as to be
scarcely capable of speaking.

He was now laid in the centre of a large conjuring
house and the same man who had deceived me in swallowing a bayonet during the summer, now offered to
swallow a piece of board about the size of a barrel stave.
This board was prepared by another man and painted,
according to the direction of the juggler, with a rude pic-
ture of some beast of prey on one side, and a resemblance
of the sky on the other.

After the conjurer had held the necessary conference
with the invisible spirits, he asked if I was present; for he
had heard of my saying that I did not see him swallow the
bayonet fair. He now desired me to come nearer, on
which the mob made a lane for me, and I advanced close

to him and found him standing as naked as he was born.

When the piece of board was delivered to him, he put it to his mouth and it apparently slipped down his throat like lightning, only leaving about three inches protruding from his lips. After walking back and forth three times, he hauled it up, and then ran into the conjuring house. Notwithstanding that I was all attention, I could not detect the deceit. As to the reality of the piece of wood, I had it in my hands both before and immediately after the ceremony.

To lessen the apparent magnitude of the miracle, and to give some colour to my scepticism, it is necessary to say that this feat was performed on a dark and exceedingly cold night and, although there was a large fire at a distance, there was still great room for collusion. Though the conjurer was naked, there were several of his fraternity, well clothed, attending close upon him.

It is necessary to observe that, on the day preceding the performance, I accidentally came on the conjurer as he was sitting under a bush several miles from camp, shaping a piece of wood exactly like the part which stuck out of his mouth after he had pretended to swallow the stave.

Not long after the above performance had taken place, some of the Indians asked me what I thought of it. I was some time at a loss for an answer, not caring to affront them by hinting my suspicions. I urged, however, the impossibility of a man swallowing a piece of wood that was not only much longer than his whole back, but nearly twice as broad as he could extend his mouth. On which some of them laughed at my ignorance, as they were pleased to call it, and said the spirits-in-waiting swallowed or otherwise concealed the stick, and only left the end sticking out of the conjurer's mouth.

My guide, Matonabbee, with all his good sense, was so bigoted in this manner that he assured me he had seen a man, who was then in our company, swallow a child's cradle with much ease. This story so far exceeded the feats which I had seen that, for the sake of keeping up the farce, I began to be very inquisitive about the spirits which appear to them on those occasions. I was told that they appeared in various shapes, for almost every conjurer had his particular attendant, but that the spirit attending the man who pretended to swallow the piece of wood, generally appeared to him in the shape of a cloud.

This I thought very apropos to the present occasion, for I must admit that I never had so thick a cloud thrown before my eyes before or since. Had it not been for the accident that I saw him make the counterpart to the piece he was said to have swallowed, I should have been still at a loss to account for so extraordinary a deception.

After our conjurer had executed his feat, he was joined inside the hut by five other men and an old woman, all great professors of the art, who stripped themselves quite naked and soon began to suck, blow, sing and dance around the poor paralytic. They continued so for three days and four nights without taking the least rest or refreshment, not even so much as a drop of water. When these poor, deluded and deluding people eventually came out of the conjuring house, their mouths were so parched from thirst as to be quite black, and their throats so sore that they were scarce able to articulate a single word.

After so long an abstinence they were careful not to eat or drink too much at one time, and indeed some of them appeared to be almost as bad as the poor man they were trying to relieve; but much of this was feigned. They lay on their backs with their eyes fixed, as if in the agonies of death, and were treated like young children. Some one sat constantly by them, moistening their mouths with fat, and now and then giving them a drop of water.

This farce only lasted for the first day, after which they seemed to be perfectly well, except for a degree of hoarseness. And it is truly wonderful, though the strictest truth, that when the poor sick man was taken from the conjuring house he had regained his appetite to an amazing degree, and was able to move all his fingers and toes on the side that had so long been dead. In three weeks he recovered so far as to be capable of walking, and at the end of six weeks he went a-hunting for his family.

He accompanied me back to Prince of Wales Fort, and since that time he has frequently visited the Factory, though he never had a healthy look afterwards and was troubled by a nervous complaint. The disorder seemed to have changed his whole character, since, before the paralytic stroke, he was distinguished for his good nature, benevolent disposition, and lack of avarice. But after this event he was the most fractious, quarrelsome, discontented, and covetous wretch alive.

Though the ordinary tricks of these conjurers may be easily detected and justly exploded, yet the apparent good effects of their labours on the sick is not so easily accounted for. Perhaps the implicit confidence placed in them by the sick people may leave the mind so perfectly at rest as to cause the disorder to take a favourable turn. In any event, a few successful cases are quite sufficient to establish the doctor's character and reputation.

When these jugglers take a dislike to, and threaten a secret revenge on some one, it often proves fatal to that person. This results from a firm belief that the conjurer has power over the threatened person's life. Sometimes a threat of this kind causes the death of a whole family, and that without any blood being shed, or the least apparent molestation being offered any of the parties.

As a proof of this, Matonabbee once informed me – after we had regained the Fort – that a man whom I had seen only once had treated him in such a manner that he was afraid for his life. Because he had always thought me possessed of the conjurers' art, Matonabbee pressed me very much to kill this fellow, though he was then at a distance of several hundred miles from us.

To please this great man to whom I owed so much, I drew a rough sketch of two human figures in a wrestling attitude. In the hand of one I drew a bayonet pointing to the breast of the other. The one with the bayonet, I told Matonabbee, was myself; the other was his enemy. Opposite these figures I drew a pine-tree, over which I placed a large human eye, and out of the tree projected a human hand.

I gave the paper to Matonabbee with instructions to make it as publicly known as possible. Sure enough, the following year Matonabbee informed me that the man had died, though at the time of death he was no less than three hundred miles from the Fort. The man had been in perfect health until he had heard of my design against him, but almost immediately afterwards he became quite gloomy and, refusing all sustenance, in a very few days died.

After this I was frequently applied to on the same account, both by Matonabbee and other leading Indians, but never thought proper to comply with their requests; by which means I not only preserved the credit I gained on the first attempt, but always kept them in awe, and in some degree of respect and obedience to me.

Thirteen

Having dried as many fish and fish roes as we could conveniently take with us, we left Anaw'd Lake on the first day of December. For thirteen days we walked in a south-westerly direction along a course of small lakes, joined to each other by little rivers or creeks. On our way we caught a few fish, and saw many beaver houses, but these had so many stones in their composition that the Indians killed but few beaver, and those only at a great expense of labour and tools.

On the 13th the Indians killed two deer, which were the first we had seen since October 20th. During that entire period of near two months, we had lived on dried meat and fish, with a few rabbits and spruce partridges. Though I and some others experienced no real want, yet there were many in our company who could scarce be said to live, and who would not have existed at all but for the dry meat we had with us.

On the 24th of December we arrived at the north side of the great Athapuscow Lake, having seen numerous woodland deer and beaver, many of which the Indians killed. The days were then so short that the sun only took a circuit of a few compass points above the horizon and did not, at its greatest altitude, rise half-way up the trees. However, the brilliance of the aurora borealis and of the stars, even without the assistance of the moon, made some amends for this deficiency. Although the Indians make no difference between night and day when they are hunting beaver, the winter nights are found insufficiently light for hunting deer or moose.

I do not remember having met with any travellers into high northern latitudes who said they had heard the northern lights make any noise. However, I can positively affirm that in still nights I have frequently heard them make a rustling and a crackling noise like the waving of a large flag in a fresh gale of wind.

The woodland deer, which are the only species found in these parts, are so much larger than those which frequent the barren grounds that a small doe is equal in size to a northern buck. The flesh of these deer is not so much esteemed as that of the barren-ground kind, for it is coarser and of a different flavour, comparing to it rather as the large Lincolnshire mutton compares to spring lamb.

The beaver being here so plentiful, the attention of my companions was chiefly engaged upon them, as they not only furnished delicious food, but their skins proved a valuable acquisition.

The situation of beaver houses varies. Where the animals are numerous they are found to inhabit lakes, ponds, and rivers as well as narrow creeks. Rivers and creeks are generally chosen if possible, for then the beavers have the advantage of a current to convey wood and other necessaries to their habitations, and because they are usually safer than houses built in standing water.

The beavers that build in small rivers or creeks, in which the water is liable to be drained off when the back supplies are dried up by the frost, are wonderfully taught by instinct to provide against this evil by making a dam across the river at a convenient distance from their houses. This I look upon as the most curious piece of workmanship that is performed by the beaver; not so much for the neatness of the work, as for its strength and real service. At the same time it discovers such a degree of sagacity and foresight in the animals as is little inferior to that of the human species.

Beaver dams differ in shape according to the nature of the place where they are built. If the water has but little motion, then the dam is almost straight across; but where the current is more rapid, the dam is curved, with its convex side toward the stream. The materials used are driftwood, green willows, and birch and poplars if they can be got; and also mud and stones intermixed. There is no regular order observable in the manner of building, except that the whole is made with a regular sweep, and all the parts are built to equal strength.

In places that have been long frequented by the beaver undisturbed, their dams become a solid bank capable of resisting a great force of water or ice. Willow, poplar and birch generally take root and, by degrees, form a regular-planted hedge which I have sometimes seen to grow so tall that birds have nested in the branches.

The houses are built of the same materials as the dams, and are proportioned in size to the numbers of the inhabitants, which seldom exceeds four old, and six to eight young ones. These houses, though not altogether unworthy of admiration, fall short of the general description given of them, for they are of a much ruder structure than the dams.

Those who have undertaken to describe the interior of the houses as having several apartments appropriated to various uses, such as eating, sleeping, storehouses, and one for natural occasions, must have been very little acquainted with their subject. I affirm that everything of the kind is absolutely devoid of truth. Notwithstanding the sagacity of these animals, it has never been observed that they aim at any other conveniences in their houses except a dry place to lie on, and a place where they can eat their victuals, which they occasionally take out of the water.

It frequently happens, however, that some of the large houses have one or more partitions; but these are no more than a part of the main building, left by the sagacity of the beaver to support the roof. These apartments, as some are pleased to call them, seldom have any communication between them except by water; so that the whole structure may be called a double or multiple house. I have seen one beaver house, built on a small island, that had near a dozen apartments under one roof and, excepting two or three, none of these communicated with the others. As there were beaver enough here to inhabit each apartment, it is probable that each family knew its own, and entered by its own door. The Indians who were with me when I saw this particular house, killed twelve old beaver and twenty-five younger ones; and several more escaped their vigilance.

Travellers who assert that the beaver have two doors to their houses, one on the landward side, and the other next to the water, must be even less acquainted with these animals. Such a proceeding would render the houses of no use, either to protect them from attacks, or against the extreme cold of winter. The quickhatches or wolverines, who are great enemies of the beaver, would not leave one of them alive if there were a passage into the houses on the landward side.

I cannot refrain from smiling when I read the accounts of authors who have written about the economy of these animals. There seems to be a contest between them as to who shall most exceed in fiction. However, the compiler of *Wonders of Nature and Art* seems, in my opinion, to have succeeded best. He has not only collected the fictions of other writers, but has so greatly improved upon them that little remains to be added to his account of the beaver – except perhaps a vocabulary of their language, a code of their laws, and a sketch of their religion.

To deny that the beaver is possessed of a very considerable degree of sagacity would be as absurd as the belief of those authors who think they cannot allow them too much. But it is somewhat difficult to conceive of a beaver (which, when standing erect, does not exceed three feet in height) "driving stakes as thick as a man's leg into the ground to a depth of three or four feet."

Their "wattling those stakes with twigs" is equally absurd, as is their "plastering the insides of their houses with a mixture of mud and straw" or "swimming with mud and stones on their tails."

When building their houses, beavers usually lay most of the wood crosswise and nearly horizontal, leaving a cavity in the middle. When any unnecessary branches project inward, they cut them off with their teeth. The whole of their houses and their dams are, from the foundations up, one general mass of wood and mud, mixed with stones if these can be procured. The mud is taken from the edge of the bank, or from the bottom of the creek or pond, near the house. Despite the small size of their fore-paws, this material is held close up between the paws, under the throat. Wood is dragged along by means of their teeth.

All their work is done at night and they are so expeditious that in the course of a single night I have known them to have collected mud amounting to thousands of little handfuls. When any mixture of straw or grass has appeared in it, this has been assuredly by merest chance. The idea that they designedly make a composition of straw and mud is void of truth.

It is the policy of these animals to cover the outside of the house with fresh mud, as late in the fall as possible, even after the frosts become pretty severe. This wet mud soon freezes and becomes so hard as to even prevent their enemy the wolverine from disturbing them during the winter.

As they are frequently seen to walk over their work and sometimes to give a flap with their tail, this has undoubtedly given rise to the vulgar opinion that they use their tail as a trowel. However, the flapping of the tail is in reality no more than a custom they indulge in when they are startled – a custom they preserve even after becoming tame and domestic.

Their chief food is a large root which grows at the bottom of lakes and rivers. They also eat bark, particularly that of the poplar, birch, and willow. In winter they store some of these barks beneath the ice, but the aforementioned roots comprise the bulk of their food in the winter season. In summer they vary their diet by eating berries and other herbage that grows near their haunts.

When the ice breaks up in spring, the beaver leave their houses and rove about for the whole summer, probably in search of more commodious situations. If they find none, they return to their old habitations a little before the fall of the leaf, and lay in their winter stock of wood and bark. They seldom begin to repair the houses until the frost commences.

When they shift their habitations, or when the increase in numbers renders it necessary to enlarge old houses, or to build new ones, they begin felling the wood for this purpose early in the summer; though they do not begin building till the middle of August.

Persons attempting to take beaver in winter should be well acquainted with their manner of life. They have many holes in the nearby banks which serve as places of retreat when an injury is offered to their houses. In general, it is in these holes that they are taken by the Indians. On a small river or creek, the Indians sometimes find it necessary to stake the river across, to prevent the animals from escaping. Afterwards they endeavour to find out all the holes or places of retreat under the banks. Each man, being furnished with an ice-chisel, lashes it to a staff four or five feet long. He then walks along the shore, knocking his chisel against the ice. Those who are well acquainted with the work can tell by the sound of the ice when they have found a beaver hole or vault. They then cut a hole through the ice, big enough to admit an old beaver.

While they are about this work, some of the women and under-strappers are busy breaking open the house. At times this is no easy task, for I have known these houses to be five or six feet thick, and one I saw was eight feet thick at the crown. But when the beavers find that their house is being invaded, they flee to the holes in the banks for shelter.

Perceiving their movements by the agitation of the water at the holes, the waiting Indians immediately block up the entrances to the vaults with stakes. They then haul the beaver out, either by hand or with a large hook fastened to the end of a stick.

In this kind of hunting each man has the sole right to all the beaver he catches in the vaults he has marked. Those beaver caught in the house also belong to those who take them.

Beaver are sometimes caught during the summer in nets, and very frequently in traps. In winter they are very fat and delicious, but the trouble of rearing their young, and their roaming about, makes them indifferent eating in the summer.

In respect to the beaver dunging in their houses, as some assert, this is quite wrong, as they always plunge into the water to do it. I am the better enabled to make this assertion having kept several of them till they became so domesticated as to answer to their names, and to follow me about as a dog would do. They were as much pleased at being fondled as any animal I ever saw.

I had a house built for them, and a small piece of water before the door into which they always plunged when they wanted to ease nature. When the weather became so cold that I was obliged to take them into the house, they always went into a large tub of water which I set for that purpose, and they made not the least dirt in the house, although they were kept in my own sitting-room.

They were such constant companions of the Indian women and children that when the Indians were away for any length of time, the beaver showed great uneasiness. On the Indians' return, the animals showed equal marks of pleasure, fondling on them, crawling into their laps, laying on their backs, sitting erect like a squirrel, and behaving to them like children who see their parents but seldom. They lived during the winter on the same food the women did, and were remarkably fond of rice and plum pudding. They would also eat partridges and fresh venison; but I never tried them with fish, which I have heard they will at times prey upon.

Fourteen

AFTER SOME days we proceeded to cross the Athapus-cow Lake; but as we lost much time hunting deer and beaver, which were very plentiful on some of the islands, it was the 9th of January before we reached the southern shore.

From the best information which I could get from the natives, this immense lake appears to be about 360 miles long from east to west, but only about sixty miles across. It is said to be narrowest at the part where we crossed it. This part is full of islands, most of which are clothed with fine tall poplars, birch, and pines, and are well stocked with woodland deer. On some of the larger islands we also found beaver living on the inland ponds, though there were none about the margins of the islands.

The lake is stored with great quantities of fine fish, particularly between the islands which, in some parts, are so close together as to form very narrow channels in which I found a considerable current setting eastward.

Besides the usual fish which are common to most of the lakes in this country, there was another which appeared peculiar to this lake. Its body resembles that of a pike in shape, but the large, stiff scales are of a beautiful bright silver colour. The mouth is large and, when open, resembles that of a sturgeon. Though without teeth, the fish takes hold as ravenously as a pike or trout. The Northern Indians call this fish *Shees*. Some of the

Athapuscow trout were the largest I ever saw, and some caught by my companions could not have been less than thirty-five or forty pounds in weight. Pike also grow to an incredible size in this water, and I have seen some that weighed upwards of forty pounds.

The scene on the south side was agreeably altered from the jumble of rocks and hills which lies to the north side of the lake. It is a fine level country, with not a hill to be seen, nor stones either; so that those of my companions who were obliged to heat water in birch-bark containers were forced to load their sledges with stones from one of the islands before we reached the mainland.

The extreme poverty of most of the Indians will not permit one half of them to purchase brass or copper pots, and so they are still under the necessity of boiling their victuals in large, upright vessels made of birch bark. As these will not stand exposure to the flames, the Indians supply the defect by heating stones red-hot, and putting them in the water until it boils. This method of cooking, though expeditious, is attended by one great evil; the heated stones are not only liable to shiver to pieces, but many being of a coarse and gritty nature, they fall into masses of gravel in the kettle. The victuals therefore, are frequently full of sand as a result.

Buffalo, moose, and beaver were very plentiful, as were the tracks of marten, foxes, and other fur animals. My companions, however, gave themselves no trouble to catch these latter, for the buffalo, moose, and beaver engaged all their attention, being of excellent flesh; while the flesh of the fox, wolf, and wolverine are never eaten by these people, except when they are in the greatest distress, and then only to save life.

Wolves are frequently met with in all the countries west of Hudson's Bay, both on the barren grounds and amongst the woods, but they are not numerous, and it is uncommon to see more than three or four of them in a herd. Those that keep amongst the woods are generally of the usual colour, but those killed by the Eskimos are perfectly white. They are all very shy of the human race, yet when sharp set, they will frequently follow the Indians for several days, though they always keep at a distance.

They are great enemies of the Indian dogs, and frequently kill and eat those that are heavy loaded and cannot keep up with the main body.

The Northern Indians have formed strange ideas of this animal, as they think it does not eat its meat raw, but by a singular and wonderful sagacity, peculiar to itself, has a method of cooking food without fire. The wolves generally lead a forlorn life all winter, and are seldom seen in pairs until spring, when they couple. They remain in pairs all summer, and burrow underground to bring forth their young.

Though it is natural to suppose them very fierce at those times, yet I have frequently seen the Indians go to their dens, take out the young ones, and play with them. I never knew a Northern Indian to hurt one of the pups; on the contrary, they always put them carefully back into the den again. I have sometimes seen them paint the faces of the young wolves with vermilion or ochre.

The woodland buffalo of these parts are in general much larger than the English black cattle; particularly the bulls. In fact these are so heavy that when six or eight Indians are in company at the skinning of a large bull, they never attempt to turn it over while entire, but when the upper side is skinned, they cut off the leg and shoulder, rip up the belly, take out the intestines, cut off the head, and make the corpse as light as possible before they turn it to skin the other side.

This skin is, in some places, of an incredible thickness; particularly about the neck, where it often exceeds an inch. The horns are short, black, and almost straight, but very thick at the roots.

The head of a bull is of great size and weight. Some I have seen were so large that I could not lift them without difficulty; but the heads of the cows are much smaller.

The hair of the body is soft and curled, somewhat approaching wool. It is generally a sandy brown, and of an equal length and thickness over the body; but on the head and neck it is much longer.

After reducing all parts of the skin to an equal thickness by scraping, the Indians dress them with the hair on, for clothing; they then become light, soft, warm, and durable. They also dress some of these skins, without the hair, into leather, from which they make tents and moccasins. However, the grain is open and spongy, and by no means equal in goodness to that of the skin of the moose.

The buffaloes chiefly delight in wide patches of plains, which in these parts produce a kind of small flags and rushes, upon which they feed. When pursued they always take to the woods. They are of such amazing strength that, when flying through the woods from a pursuer, they frequently brush down trees as thick as a man's arm. Be the snow ever so deep, such is their agility and strength that they are enabled to plunge through it faster than the swiftest Indian can run on snowshoes. I have been an eyewitness to this many times. Once, indeed, I had the vanity to think I could keep pace with them for I was at that time celebrated for being particularly fleet of foot on snowshoes. I soon found that I was no match for the buffaloes, notwithstanding that they were plunging through such deep snow that their bellies made a trench in it as large as if many heavy sacks had been hauled through it.

Of all the large beasts in these parts, the buffalo is the easiest to kill, and the moose the most difficult. Neither are the woodland deer very easy to approach, except in windy weather, and even then it requires much practice and a good deal of patience to slay them.

The flesh of the buffalo is exceedingly good eating, and so free of disagreeable smell or taste that is resembles beef as nearly as possible. The flesh of the cows, when some time gone with calf, is reckoned the finest; and the young calves, cut out of the mothers' bellies, are reckoned a great delicacy indeed.

The hunch on their shoulders is not a large, fleshy lump as some suppose, but is occasioned by the bones which form the withers being continued to a greater length than in any other animal. The flesh surrounding this part, being equally intermixed with fat and lean, is reckoned among the nicest bits. The tongue is also very delicate and, what is most extraordinary, when the beasts are in the poorest state, the tongue remains fine and fat.

The moose is also a large beast, exceeding the largest horse in height, bulk, and the length of the legs. The bulk of the body, the shortness of the neck, and the uncommon length of head and ears, combined with an entire lack of tail, give them a very awkward appearance.

Their legs are so long, and their necks so short, that they cannot graze at ground level like other animals, but are obliged to browse on the tops of large plants and on the leaves of trees during the summer. In winter they feed on the tops of willows and the small branches of the birch tree.

In summer they generally frequent the banks of rivers and lakes, probably to avoid the flies and mosquitoes by getting into the water. They are also fond of a variety of water plants, which is a nice adaptation, for they can browse on these while being almost completely submerged in water, and so avoid the torment of the flies.

Their faculty of hearing is very acute, which makes them difficult to kill, especially as the Indians have no other method in winter than creeping after them until they get within gunshot. In summer, however, they are frequently killed while crossing rivers or swimming lakes. When pursued on water they are the most inoffensive of all animals, never making any resistance. The young ones are so simple that I have seen an Indian paddle up to one and take it by its poll. The poor, harmless animal seemed as contented as if swimming alongside its dam, looking up into our eyes with the fearless innocence of a house-lamb, and using its forefeet to clear the mosquitoes out of its eyes.

I have seen women and boys kill moose in the water by knocking them on the head with a hatchet. Once I saw two boys, who were without gun or bow or hatchet, kill a moose by forcing a stick up its fundament.

Common deer are much more dangerous to approach in a canoe, for they kick up their hind legs with such violence as to endanger any birch-bark craft that comes within reach.

Moose are also the easiest to tame and domesticate of any of the deer kind. I have repeatedly seen them at Churchill as tame as sheep, and more so, for they would follow their keeper any distance from home, and never offer to deviate from the path.

A tame moose was safely shipped to England for His Majesty, from Churchill; but a second one – a young male – died aboard the ship.

The flesh of the moose is very good, though the grain is coarse, and it is much tougher than any other kind of venison. The nose is most excellent, as is also the tongue. It is perhaps worth remarking that the livers of moose are never found, and that, like the deer, they have no gall. The fat of the intestines is hard, like suet; but the external fat is soft, like that of a breast of mutton.

In all their actions they appear very uncouth, and when disturbed they never run, but make a kind of trot, which their long legs enable them to do with ease and swiftness.

Dressed moose-skins make excellent tent-covers and moccasin leather, and in fact every kind of clothing. The Indian women render them as soft as a piece of thick cloth, but unless they are dressed in oil they grow hard after being wet.

Though the flesh of the moose is esteemed by most Indians, yet the Northern Indians did not reckon either it or the buffalo flesh to be substantial food. This, I think, was entirely from prejudice, for the Northern Indians have a very strong predilection for the deer of the barren ground.

Soon after our arrival at the south shore of Athapuscow Lake, Matonabbee proposed continuing our course to the south-west in hopes of meeting some of the Athapuscow Indians. This was agreeable to me, for I wished if possible to purchase a tent and some ready-dressed skins from them. We were then in great want of tents and moccasin leather for, though my companions were daily killing moose and buffalo, the weather was so cold as to render dressing the skins impracticable.

To dress these skins according to the Indian method, a lather is made from the brains and some of the softest fat or marrow of the animal, in which the skin is well soaked. It is then taken out and dried by the heat of the fire and then hung up in the smoke for several days. On being taken down again, it is soaked and washed in warm water until the grain of the skin is perfectly open and has imbibed a sufficient amount of water. It is then wrung out and dried before a slow fire, care being taken to rub and stretch it as long as any moisture remains in the skin. By this simple method some of the skins can be made very delicate, both to the eye and to the touch.

While out hunting on January 11th, some of my companions saw the track of a strange snowshoe. They followed it, and at a considerable distance came to a little hut where they discovered a young woman sitting quite alone. As she understood their language, they brought her back to our camp.

On examination she proved to be one of the western Dog-ribbed Indians who had been taken prisoner by the Athapuscows in the summer of 1770. The following summer, when the Indians who took her were near this part, she eloped from them with intent to return to her own country. However, the distance was so vast, and she had been carried such a great way by canoe along the twistings and turnings of the rivers and lakes, that she had forgotten the way to her home. She therefore built the hut in which we found her, and here she had resided from the first setting-in of fall.

From her account of the moons which had passed since

her elopement, it appeared the she had been near seven months without seeing a human face. During this time she had supported herself very well by snaring partridge, rabbits and squirrels, and she had also killed two or three beaver and some porcupines. That she had not been in want was evident from the fact that she still had a small store of provisions by her when she was discovered. She was in good health and condition, and I think was one of the finest Indian women that I have seen in any part of North America.

The methods practised by this poor creature to procure a livelihood were truly admirable. When the few deer sinews that she had taken with her were all expended in making snares, and sewing her clothing, she had nothing with which to replace them but the sinews of rabbits' legs and feet. These she twisted together with great dexterity and success. The rabbits, and other things that she caught in her snares, not only furnished her with a comfortable subsistence but also with enough skins to make a warm and neat suit of winter clothing.

It is scarcely possible to think that a person in her forlorn situation could be so composed as to contrive, or execute, anything not absolutely essential to her existence. Nevertheless, all her clothing, besides being calculated for real service, showed great taste and no little variety of ornament. The materials, though rude, were very curiously wrought, and so judiciously placed as to make the whole of her garb have a very pleasing and rather romantic appearance.

Her leisure hours from hunting had been employed in twisting the inner rind or bark of willows into small lines, like net-twine, of which she had some hundred fathoms. With this she intended to weave a fishing net as soon as the spring advanced. It is the custom of the Dog-ribbed Indians to make their nets in this manner, and they are much preferable to the deer-thong nets of the Northern Indians which, although they appear very good when dry, grow so soft and slippery in the water that the hitches are apt to slip and let the fish escape. They are also liable to rot, unless frequently taken out of the water and dried.

Five or six inches of an iron hoop, made into a knife, and the shank of an arrow-head of iron, which served as an awl, were all the metals this poor woman had. However, with these simple implements she had made herself complete snowshoes and several other useful articles.

Her method of making a fire was equally singular, since she had no materials for the purpose other than two hard, sulphurous rocks. By long friction and hard knocking, she made these produce a few sparks which she communicated to some touchwood. However, as this method was attended by great trouble, and was not always certain of success, she did not suffer her fire to go out all that winter. Hence we may conclude that she did not know how to produce fire by friction, as is done amongst the Eskimos and many other uncivilized nations.

The singularity of her circumstances, the comeliness of her person, and her proved accomplishments, occasioned a strong contest between several of the Indians of my party as to who should have her for a wife. The poor girl was actually won and lost at wrestling by half a score of different men that same evening.

Even Matonabbee, who at that time had seven grown women as wives, besides a young girl of eleven or twelve years, would have put in for the prize had not one of his wives made him ashamed by telling him that he already had more wives than he could attend to. Unfortunately this piece of satire proved fatal to the wife who made it, for Matonabbee, who would have liked to be thought equal to eight or ten men in every respect, took it as a serious affront. He fell upon the poor wife with both hands and feet, and bruised her to such a degree that, after lingering some time, she died.

When the Athapuscows took the Dog-ribbed woman prisoner, they did it, according to universal custom, by surprising her and her party in the night, and killed every soul except her and three other young women. Among those whom they killed were her father, mother, and husband. She concealed her young child in a bundle of clothes, and took it with her undiscovered. But when she arrived at the place where the Athapuscow men had left their wives, these began to examine her bundle. Discovering the child, one of the women took it from her and killed it on the spot.

This last piece of barbarity gave her such a disgust of these Indians that, notwithstanding her captor treated her in every respect as a wife and was, she admitted, remarkably kind to, and even fond of her, she could never reconcile herself to the tribe. Instead she chose to expose herself to misery and want, rather than live in ease and affluence among people who had so cruelly murdered her infant. The poor woman's relation of this shocking story, which she delivered in a very affecting manner, only excited laughter amongst the savages of my party.

When we conversed with the woman soon afterwards, she told us that her country lay so far to the westward that she had never seen iron or any other kind of metal until she was taken prisoner. All of her tribe, she observed, made their hatchets and ice-chisels of deer horn, and their knives of stone or bones. The only instruments they employed to work wood were beaver's teeth. Though they had heard of the useful materials with which the nations to the east of them were supplied by the English, they were actually obliged to retreat farther west in order to avoid the Athapuscow Indians, who made surprising slaughter among them both in winter and summer.

It is too common a case with most of the tribes of Southern Indians for the women to desire their husbands or friends, on going to war, to bring them back a slave so they can have the pleasure of killing it. Some of these inhuman women will even accompany their husbands, and murder the women and children as fast as their husbands do the men.

When I was at Cumberland House I was acquainted with a young lady of this extraordinary turn. When I desired some Indians that were going to war to bring me back a young slave that I could bring up as a domestic, Miss was equally desirous that one be brought to her for the cruel purpose of murdering it. It is scarcely possible to express my astonishment at hearing such a request from a young creature scarce sixteen years of age. When I had recovered from my surprise, I ordered her to leave the settlement; which she did – with those who were going to war. It is therefore likely that she was not disappointed in her desire.

Fifteen

ON THE SIXTEENTH of January, 1772, we reached the grand Athapuscow River, which is about two miles wide near where it empties itself into the great lake of the same name. The woods nearby, particularly the pines and poplars, are the tallest and stoutest I have seen in any part of North America.

The bank of the river is very high, sometimes a hundred feet above the water; but the soil is loamy and very subject to moulder away in the heavy summer rains. At the time of the break-up of the ice it is not uncommon, so I am told, to see whole points of land washed away by the inundations, while vast numbers of trees are hurled down the stream. On the shores and islands of the lake was the greatest quantity of driftwood I ever saw, and some of the wood was large enough for the masts of the largest ships that are built.

Besides the Athapuscow, there are several other rivers of less note which empty into the great lake. There are also creeks and rivers on the north-east side, some of which, after much wandering through the barren grounds, discharge into larger rivers that eventually find their way to the northern part of Hudson's Bay some hundreds of miles from Churchill River.

We continued south along the Athapuscow River for many days, but, though we passed several of the former winter haunts of the Athapuscow Indians, we saw no trace of people having been there this season. During the preceding summer they had set fire to the woods, and notwithstanding the deep snow, and the many months which had elapsed, the fires were still burning in many places, so that we often imagined we were seeing the smoke of camp fires.

Our expectations thus disappointed, we resolved to spend as much time as we could in hunting beaver, buffalo and moose, so that we might be able to reach Prince of Wales Fort a little before the usual time for ships arriving from England. Accordingly, on the 27th of January, we struck off to the eastward, leaving the river where it trends due south.

Game of all kinds being most plentiful, we made but short days' journeys, often remaining in one spot for two or three days to eat up the spoils of the chase. The woods through which we passed were often so thick that it was necessary to cut a path, before the women could pass with the sledges. In other places the woods had formerly been set on fire and burnt, so that we had to walk great distances to find green brush enough to floor our tents.

On February 24th, we encountered a strange Northern Indian leader called Thlewsanellie who, with his band, joined us from the eastward. He presented Matonabbee and myself with a foot of tobacco each, and a two-quart keg of brandy which he had intended as a gift to the Southern Indians. The tobacco was very acceptable but, not having tasted liquor for so long, I would not take any of the brandy but left it to the Indians, who were so numerous that there was scarcely a taste for each. Few of the Northern Indians who keep at a distance from the Fort, are fond of spirits; but those who shoot geese for us in spring will drink it at free cost as fast as the Southern Indians do – though few of them are so imprudent as to buy it.

We were now travelling on a little river that empties into Lake Clowey, and it being well stocked with beaver ponds, and the land abounding with moose and buffalo, we made but slow progress in our journey. Many days were spent hunting, feasting, and drying a large amount of buffalo flesh to carry with us, for my companions knew that a few days' walk to the eastward would bring us to a part where we would not see any of these animals.

Thlewsanellie and his party told us that all was well at the Fort when they left it, which must have been about the 5th of November in 1771. Most of them now proceeded northwestward, but some, who had procured furs in the early part of the winter, joined our party.

Setting off to the south-east on the 28th, we now proceeded at a much greater rate, since little or no time was lost in hunting. The next day we came on the tracks of strangers, and some of my companions were at pains to search them out. Finding them to be poor, inoffensive people, they plundered them of the few furs they had, together with one young woman.

Every additional act of violence, committed by my companions on the poor and the distressed, served to increase my indignation and dislike. This last act, however, displeased me more than all their former actions because it was committed on a set of harmless creatures whose general manner of life renders them the most secluded from society of any of the human race.

The people of this family, as it may be called, have for a generation past taken up their abode in some woods which are situated so far out on the barren grounds as to be quite out of the track of other Indians. This place is some hundreds of miles distant both from the main woods and from the sea. Few of the trading Northern Indians have ever visited it, but those who have give a most pleasing description of it. It is situated on the banks of a river which has communications with several fine lakes. As the current sets north-eastward, it empties itself, in all probability, into some part of Hudson's Bay, probably into Baker Lake at the head of Chesterfield Inlet.

The accounts given of this place, and of the manner of life of its inhabitants, would fill a volume. Let it suffice to observe that it is remarkably favourable for every kind of game that the barren ground produces. However, the seasonal continuance of game is somewhat uncertain, which being the case, the few people who compose this little commonwealth are, by long custom and the constant example of their forefathers, possessed of a provident turn of mind, together with a degree of frugality unknown to every other tribe in this country except the Eskimos.

Deer are said to visit their country in astonishing numbers both in spring and autumn. The inhabitants kill and dry as much deer flesh as possible, particularly in the fall, so they are seldom in want of a good winter's stock.

Geese, ducks and swans visit them in great plenty during their migrations, and are caught in considerable numbers in snares. It is also reported (though I doubt the truth of it) that a remarkable species of partridge, as big as English fowls, are found in that part of the country only. These, it is said, as well as common partridges, are killed in great numbers with snares as well as with bows and arrows.

The rivers and lakes near the little forest where the family has fixed its abode, abound with fine fish that are easily caught with hooks and nets. In fact, I have not seen or heard of any part of this country which seems to possess half the advantages requisite for a constant residence, that are ascribed to this little spot.

The descendants of the present inhabitants, however, must in time evacuate it for want of wood, which is of so slow a growth in these regions. What is used in one year, exclusive of what is carried away by Eskimos who resort to this place for lumber, must cost many years to replace.

It may be thought strange that any part of such a happily situated community should be found so far away from their home. Indeed, nothing but necessity could possibly have urged them to undertake a journey of so many hundred miles as they had done. But no situation is without its inconvenience, and their woods containing few, if any, birch trees, they had come so far to procure birch bark for canoes, as well as some of the fungus that grows on the birch tree and is used for tinder.

By the first of March we were leaving the fine, level country of the Athapuscows and approaching the stony mountains and hills which bound the Northern Indian country. Moose and beaver were still plentiful, but we saw no more buffaloes.

On the 14th we came up to more strangers, and amongst them was a man who, in March of 1771, had been entrusted with a letter from me to Prince of Wales Fort. He had with him an answer, dated the 21st of June. When he had received the letter from me, we had been very uncertain what route we should take on our return from the Coppermine River, and in all probability he had not then determined where he himself would spend the present winter. Consequently our meeting each other was by the greatest accident.

These Indians also joined our party, which now consisted of twenty tents and about two hundred persons. Indeed our party had never been much less during the whole winter.

I cannot sufficiently lament the loss of my quadrant, as the want of it must render our course from Point Lake very uncertain. My watch stopping at the Athapuscow Lake contributed greatly to the misfortune, as I was then deprived of every means of estimating the distance we walked with any degree of accuracy, particularly in thick weather when the sun could not be seen.

The Indians were now employed at all convenient times in procuring birch bark and making woodwork ready for building canoes, and preparing birch-wood staffs to serve as tent poles in the summer on the barren ground. None of these incidental tasks interfered with the progress of our journey. Provisions being plentiful, and the weather fine, we advanced a little each day, and on the 19th of March took up our lodgings by the side of Wholdyeah-chuck'd Whoie, or Large Pike Lake.

On the 20th we crossed this lake, which at that part was no more than seven miles wide, though it is much longer from north-west to south-east. The following day we arrived at Bedodid Lake which, in general, is not more than three miles wide, but is upward of forty miles long, which gives it the appearance of a river.

The thaws now began to be very considerable, and the underwoods were so thick as to render travelling through them difficult. We therefore walked on the ice of Bedodid Lake as long as it lay nearly in the direction of our course. After twenty-two miles we had to leave it, and fourteen miles farther east we reached Nooshetht Whoie, or Hill Island Lake.

From the 28th to the 31st of March, we were inconvenienced by a gale of wind which was so strong as to make walking on lakes or open plains impossible, and the violence of which blew down many trees and made walking in the woods somewhat dangerous.

At the beginning of April the thaw was still not general, but in the middle of each day it was considerable. It commonly froze hard at nights, and the young men took advantage of the crusted snow in the morning to run down many moose. In such a situation a man with snowshoes will scarcely make an impression in the snow, while moose and even the deer will break through up to the belly at every step. Moose are so tender-footed and short-winded that a good runner will generally tire them in less than a day, and frequently in six or eight hours. When the poor moose are incapable of further speed, they stand and keep their pursuer at bay with their head and forefeet, in the use of which they are very dexterous. The Indians, who usually carry neither bows nor guns with them on these long runs, are generally obliged to lash their knives to the ends of long sticks and stab the moose from a distance. Some of the boys and foolhardy young men, who have attempted to rush in upon them, have received such unlucky blows from the forefeet as to render their recovery very doubtful.

The flesh of the moose thus killed is bad tasting and probably unwholesome, from being overheated. The fever resulting from hours of running makes the flesh clammy, with a very disagreeable flavour resembling neither fish, flesh nor fowl. I have heard Indians say that after a long chase the moose does not produce more than a quart of blood; the rest is all settled in its flesh, which in that state must taste ten times worse than the spleen or milt of a bacon hog.

Sixteen

ON THE SEVENTH of April we crossed a part of the Theleweyaza River, at which time the deer were remarkably plentiful; but the moose had become very scarce and we had killed none since the 3rd of the month.

On the 12th we saw several swans flying northward. These were the first birds of passage we had seen that spring, except a few snowbirds, which always precede the other migrants and so are, with much propriety, called the harbingers of spring.

On the 14th, we arrived at another part of the Theleweyaza and pitched our tents near some families of Northern Indians who had been there some time snaring deer.

Despite the fact that these strangers were so poor as not to have one gun amongst them, the villains of my crew were so far from assisting them as to rob them of almost every useful article in their possession. To complete their cruelty, the men joined themselves in parties of six, eight, or ten to a gang, and dragged several of the young women from the camps of the strangers to a little distance from the tents. Here they not only ravished them, but otherwise ill-treated them in so barbarous a manner as to endanger the lives of one or two of them.

Humanity on this, as well as on other occasions during my residence among these wretches, prompted me to upbraid them for their barbarity. My remonstrances not only failed to have the desired effect, but the Indians made no scruple of telling me in the plainest terms that, if any female relation of mine had been present, she would have been served in the same manner.

Deer being plentiful, we remained at this place for ten days in order to prepare a quantity of meat and fat to carry with us, as this was the last time the Indians expected to see such plenty until we met the deer again out on the barren grounds. During our stay here, the Indians also completed the woodwork for their canoes, and procured tent poles.

While we were employed about this business the thaw became so great that the bare ground began to appear in many places, and the ice in the shallow parts of the rivers, where there was a rapid current, now began to break up. This put us in daily expectation of seeing geese, ducks, and other birds of passage.

We set out again on the 25th of April, and that day walked twenty miles to the eastward but, as some of the women had not joined us, we did not move again for two days. Then, having mustered all our forces, we moved forward and passed Theleweyaza Yeth, the place at which we had prepared woodwork for the canoes in the spring of the previous year.

The first of May dawned fair and pleasant, with a great thaw, and we had walked eight or nine miles when a heavy fall of snow came on, followed by a hard gale of wind from the northwest. At the time the bad weather struck us we were on top of a high barren hill, a considerable distance from any woods. Judging the wind to be no more than a passing squall, we sat down in expectation of its soon going by. However, as the night advanced, the gale increased to such a degree that it was impossible for a man to stand upright. We were obliged to lie down, without any other defence against the weather than putting our sledges and other lumber to windward of us. This was of little service, as it only harboured a great drift of snow with which we were soon covered to a depth of two or three feet. As the night was not very cold

I then found myself, with many of the others, lying in a puddle of water caused by the heat of our bodies melting the snow.

Fortunately the next day brought fine weather and warm sunshine and, having dried our clothing, we proceeded with our journey. Until the 5th we made good distances, but that day was so hot and sultry that we only walked thirteen miles and then halted near the same Black Bear Hill which we had seen in the spring of the previous year.

The following day we heard that there were some strange Indians, bound for the Fort with furs, in our vicinity. On hearing this, Matonabbee sent a messenger to desire their company. They soon joined us, as it is a universal practice with the Indian leaders bound toward the Factory to use their influence in canvassing for companions; they find that a large gang gains them increased respect. Indeed most of the Europeans who are resident in these parts, being utterly unacquainted with the manners and customs of the Indians, have conceived so high an opinion of these Leaders, and of their authority, as to imagine that all who accompany them are devoted to their service and command all the year. This is, in fact, so far from being the case that the authority of these great men, when absent from the Factory, never extends beyond their own families. The trifling respect shown them by their countrymen during their residence at the Fort proceeds only from motives of self-interest.

The Leaders have a disagreeable task to perform on reaching the Factory, for they are not only obliged to be the mouthpieces, but the beggars as well, for all their friends and relations, as well as for those whom they have reason to fear.

If the Governor denies them anything they ask, though it be only something to give away to the most worthless of their gang, they turn sulky and impertinent to the highest degree, no matter how rational they may be at other times. Even if they have already received five times the value of their furs, they never cease begging, and few of them ever go away satisfied.

As proof of what I assert, there was an instance when my guide, Matonabbee, arrived at the Fort at the head of a large gang of Indians, at a time when I was in command there. After the usual ceremonies I dressed him out as a Captain of the first rank, and also clothed his six wives from top to toe. But during the remainder of his stay he begged seven Lieutenants' coats, fifteen common coats, eighteen hats, eighteen shirts, eight guns, 140 pounds of gunpowder, with shot and flints in proportion; together with many hatchets, ice-chisels, files, bayonets, knives, a great quantity of tobacco, and innumerable other articles, to the total value of seven hundred beaver. And *all* of this was to give away to his followers, being exclusive of his own present, which consisted of a variety of goods to the value of four hundred beaver.

But the most extraordinary of his demands was for twelve pounds of powder, some shot and ball, tobacco, and other things, to give to two men who had hauled his tent and other lumber during the winter. I thought this demand unreasonable, and I hesitated to comply with it, hinting that he was the person who ought to satisfy these men. He immediately replied that he did not expect to be *denied such a trifle as that was*, and for the future he would carry his goods where he could get his own price for them. I was then glad to comply with his demands; but I think the incident is revealing of an Indian's conscience.

Matonabbee, and the other Indians who were bound for the Fort, now decided to leave the elderly people and young children behind, in the care of some Indians who had orders to proceed to Cathawhachaga on the barren grounds. There they were to await the return of the trading party from the Factory.

We resumed our journey on the 11th of May, at a much brisker pace, and that night pitched our tents beside the Dubawnt River. This day most of us threw away our snowshoes, but our sledges were occasionally serviceable for some time to come, particularly when we walked on the ice of rivers and lakes.

On the 12th, we halted to build canoes. These were completed on the 18th, and we continued along the ice of the Dubawnt River. By the 21st we had crossed the north-west bay of Wholdyah'd Lake, and on this day several of the Indians were forced to turn back by a shortage of provisions. Indeed, game of all sorts was so scarce that, with the exception of a few geese, we had killed nothing from the time of our leaving the women and children.

On the 22nd we killed four deer, but our numbers were still so large that these scarcely afforded us a single meal. On the 25th we crossed Snowbird Lake and at night got clear of the woods, and lay on the barren ground. This day a number of Indians struck off on a different route, not being able to proceed further with us for want of ammunition.

As we had been making good journeys for some days past, and at the same time were heavy laden, and in great distress for want of provisions, some of my companions were now so weak that they were obliged to leave their bundles of furs. Many others were so reduced as to be no longer capable of continuing with us. Being without guns or ammunition, they had become completely dependent on the fish they could catch; and though fish were pretty plentiful hereabouts, they were not always to be relied upon for such an immediate supply of food as these poor people needed.

Though I still had a sufficient stock of ammunition to serve me and all my own companions to the Fort, yet self-preservation is the first law of nature. I therefore thought it advisable to reserve the greater part of this ammunition for our own use, especially as geese and other smaller birds were the only game we met, and these bear hard on supplies of powder and shot. Most of the Indians who accompanied me the whole way had enough ammunition remaining to enable them to travel; but of the others, though we assisted many of them, yet several of their women died from want.

It is a melancholy truth, and a disgrace to what little humanity these people possess, to think that in times of want the poor women always come off short, and many of them are permitted to starve while the males are amply provided for.

We continued our course eastward and crossed the Cathawhachaga River on the 30th of May. Soon after the last person had crossed it, the ice broke up. Then, perceiving the approach of bad weather, we made what preparations our situation would admit. The rain soon began to descend in torrents that made the river overflow, to such a degree as to convert our first place of retreat into an open sea and oblige us – in the middle of the night – to assemble at the top of an adjacent hill. The violence of the wind would not allow us to pitch a tent, and the only shelter we could obtain was to take the tent-cloth over our shoulders and sit with our backs to the wind.

In this situation we were obliged to remain, without any refreshment, for three full days, until the weather moderated somewhat on the 3rd of June. Early that morning we continued our journey, but the wet and cold I had experienced in the preceding days had so benumbed my lower extremities as to render walking very troublesome for some time.

From the 3rd to the 8th we killed sufficient geese to preserve our lives, but on the 8th we at last perceived plenty of deer and the Indians shot five. This put us into good spirits again, and the number of deer we saw afforded us hopes of more plentiful times during the remainder of our journey.

We expended a little time in eating, and then in slicing some of the meat, but the drying of it occasioned no delay, as it was fastened to the women's bundles where it dried in the sun and wind while we were walking. Strange as it may appear, meat thus prepared is not only very substantial food, but pleasant to the taste. It is much esteemed by the natives, and I have found that I could travel farther on a meal of it than upon any other kind of food.

The dried meat of the Southern Indians is prepared differently, for it is exposed to the heat of a large fire which exhausts all the fine juices from it; by the time it is dry enough to prevent putrefaction, it becomes very poor. It cannot be compared with meat cured in the sun and wind, or by the heat of a very slow fire. Most Europeans, however, are fonder of the meat prepared by the Southern Indians.

On the 9th of June we spoke with many Northern Indians who were bound for Knapp's Bay to meet the trading sloop from Churchill. Having some time before taken up goods on trust from the Prince of Wales Fort, they were now taking their furs to Knapp's Bay to delay the payment of their debts. Frauds of this kind have been practised by many of these people with great success; by which means debts to a considerable amount are annually lost to the Company.

We did not lose much time in conversation with these Indians but proceeded to the south-east, and for many days afterwards we had the good fortune to meet with plenty of provisions and remarkably fine and pleasant weather. It was as if the country was desirous to make amends for the severe cold, hunger, and excessive hardships we had suffered, and which had reduced us to the greatest misery and want.

On the 18th, we arrived at Egg River and I sent a letter off post-haste to the Chief at Prince of Wales Fort, advising him of my being so far advanced on my return. On the 26th we ferried over Seal River, and on the morning of the 29th of June, 1772, I arrived again at Prince of Wales Fort.

I had been absent eighteen months and twenty-three days on this, my third expedition; but it was two years and seven months since I had first set out to find Coppermine River.

After his return from the Coppermine River, Hearne served as mate of the brigantine *Charlotte* and then was sent inland from York Factory in 1774 to establish Cumberland House, in what is now east-central Saskatchewan.

Two years later he was recalled to take command of Fort Prince of Wales and he was still master there when the Fort was attacked by a French naval force in 1782. The French had four hundred men, and Hearne had thirty-nine. He had no choice but to surrender. He was taken prisoner to France, only to be ransomed and returned to his command the following year.

He went home to England for the last time in 1787, and in 1792 he died of dropsy – aged forty-seven years.

BOOKS BY FARLEY MOWAT

People of the Deer (1952, revised edition 1975)
The Regiment (1955, new edition 1973)
Lost in the Barrens (1956)
The Dog Who Wouldn't Be (1957)
Grey Seas Under (1959)
The Desperate People (1959, revised edition 1975)
Owls in the Family (1961)
The Serpent's Coil (1961)
The Black Joke (1962)
Never Cry Wolf (1963, new edition 1973)
Westviking (1965)
The Curse of the Viking Grave (1966)
Canada North (illustrated edition 1967)
Canada North Now (revised paperback edition 1976)
This Rock Within the Sea (with John de Visser)
(1968, reissued 1976)
The Boat Who Wouldn't Float
(1969, illustrated edition 1974)
Sibir (1970, new edition 1973)
A Whale for the Killing (1972)
Wake of the Great Sealers
(with David Blackwood) (1973)
The Snow Walker (1975)
And No Birds Sang (1979)
*The World of Farley Mowat, a selection
from his works*
(edited by Peter Davison) (1980)
Sea of Slaughter (1984)
My Discovery of America (1985)
Virunga: The Passion of Dian Fossey (1987)
The New Founde Land (1989)

EDITED BY FARLEY MOWAT
Coppermine Journey (1958)

THE TOP OF THE WORLD TRILOGY
Ordeal by Ice (1960, revised edition 1973)
The Polar Passion (1967, revised edition 1973)
Tundra (1973)

M&S

THE REGIMENT
by Farley Mowat
Heroism and horror during the Italian campaign of WWII.
"Few novels can match this book for sheer excitement and
suspense." - *London Free Press*
0-7710-6694-5 $8.95 Includes 17 pages of maps

CHARLES
A Biography
by Anthony Holden
"A well-written, reflective analysis of a complex man, bewil-
dered by a life he doesn't want." - *Ottawa Citizen*
0-7710-4194-2 $6.95 Includes 32 pages of photos

LADYBUG, LADYBUG...
by W.O. Mitchell
"Funny, frightening and enlightening, a treat for Mitchell
fans." - *Halifax Daily News*
0-7710-6076-9 $5.95

WELCOME TO FLANDERS FIELDS
by Daniel G. Dancocks
A spellbinding account of the men and events in the battle that
became a benchmark of Canadian history.
0-7710-2546-7 $5.95 Includes 16 pages of photos

ABOVE TOP SECRET
The Worldwide UFO Cover-up
by Timothy Good
The most comprehensive and authoritative book on UFOs
ever written.
0-7710-3364-8 $7.95

More Great Titles from M&S Paperbacks...

PLATINUM BLUES
by William Deverell
Step behind the scenes of the gritty, no-holds-barred world of rock music in this tension-packed new thriller from the author of **Needles**.
0-7710-2662-5 $5.95

NIGHTS BELOW STATION STREET
by David Adams Richards
"A voice to be reckoned with." - *Globe and Mail*
A powerful tale of family conflict, vividly set in New Brunswick. Winner of the Governor General's award for fiction.
0-7710-7461-1 $5.95

NOW BACK TO YOU DICK
by Dick Irvin
"He writes, he scores!" - *Montreal Gazette*
The famous broadcaster gives an insider's view of some of hockey's most thrilling moments.
0-7710-4354-6 $5.95 Includes 32 pages of photos

ROBINSON FOR THE DEFENCE
by Larry Robinson with Chrys Goyens
A first-person look at the NHL by professional hockey's best defenceman.
0-7710-7551-0 $5.95 Includes 16 pages of photos

THE CANADIAN ESTABLISHMENT, Vol. 1
by Peter C. Newman
"An astonishing book...a fascinating encyclopedia...a Canadian who's who." - *Toronto Star*
0-7710-6777-1 $7.95

JOURNEY
by James A. Michener
From the master story teller, a terrific tale of five goldseekers' gruelling travels in Canada's north.
0-7710-5866-7 $5.95